SATYA MEV JAYATE

TRUTH ALONE TRIUMPHS

notionpress.com

SATYA MEV JAYATE

TRUTH ALONE TRIUMPHS

R. SELVA KUMAR

notionpress.com

Notion Press

Old No. 38, New No. 6
McNichols Road, Chetpet
Chennai - 600 031

First Published by Notion Press 2016

ISBN 978-93-86073-90-7

Dedication

This book is dedicated to (late) VIJAYKUMAR (BAJJI)

Introduction

CHAOS THEORY

It speculates that the smallest of events can have the biggest of consequences. It has been said that something as small as the flutter of a butterfly's wing can ultimately cause a tornado half-way around the world.

NEWTON'S THIRD LAW

For every action, there is an equal and opposite reaction. Similarly, for every action of human beings, there is an equal and opposite reaction, upon other living beings of this planet.

Cigarette smoking is injurious to health and wealth. Deforestation and cutting down of trees is injurious to health and wealth of our Mother Earth.

As an author, there is nothing much to tell about myself. I am the son of a farmer, who still lives as a farmer in Bangalore city. This is for the readers to know, as to what inspired me to write this story. I am not considering this story as a novel story, because in novels, the writers usually blend the language, description of characters, situations and description of actions and emotions very perfectly, but I am not a good novelist. Nevertheless, I am sure that I am a good story teller. And I am writing this story to elaborate on a simple message—"TRUTH IS GOD", "TRUTH IS NATURE" and "TRUTH ALWAYS WINS."

Since the story starts in Bangalore and revolves around this city, it is better to know a little about it. I was born, brought up and educated in Bangalore and yet I haven't traveled more than forty kilometers outside Bangalore city since the last twenty-eight years. Yet, I love the city very much, more than any other city in the country.

Bangalore city was once called as THE GARDEN CITY and THE PENSIONER'S PARADISE, but now the city has got a new name; it is called as the SILICON CITY and CONCRETE CITY. There is an old saying—"What's in a name?" but here, by the name you can judge the city's transformation over the years. Earlier, Bangalore city was called as 'The Garden City' of the country because of its trees, plantations, gardens, parks, lakes and agricultural fields. Bangalore city was also known as 'The Pensioner's Paradise' because the senior citizens of the country would settle down here after their service or retirement. They would come here for its moderate climate and pollution-free environment, which best suited the older generation. Now, the city's people are proud that the city is developing and that it has got new names like 'Silicon City' and 'Concrete City.' The city is slowly losing the golden names attached to the city.

The greenery of the city, which was once abundant, can now be seen only in Army's land, Lal Bagh and in Cubbon Park. In the name of development, the government departments and the people of the city are destroying the greenery and the cultivation lands surrounding the city. The greenery and the cultivation lands, which are rich in soil and minerals, are being converted into concrete infrastructures like buildings and roads. These concrete roads do not allow rain water to enter the earth's crust and thus cause a decrease in the ground-water level and an increase in the atmospheric temperature.

Before reading the story in this book, let us understand:

1. Some of the basic relations between science and truth.
2. Some of the greatest inventions of science, and how the inventions later altered the course of the world.
3. The aspects of the holy books.

For Hindus, their holy book is the BHAGAVATH GITA; for Christians, their holy book is the BIBLE; for Muslims, their holy book is the QURAN, and similarly for every religion there is a holy book. In all these holy books, the gods are different from one another in appearance and so are the cultures, customs, rituals, behaviors, offerings and the prayers. Even though God is different in many aspects in the holy books, His teachings are common—that in the final chapter no matter what, truth always triumphs, i.e. good wins against bad, God wins against evil. This implies that prevailing of truth is common in all the holy books and also, truth is considered as the primary God in all the holy books. There is not a single holy book or God that is against truth. From this, we can conclude that truth is the common God for all the religions or human beings.

To know and understand the meaning of truth, you have to read the story in this book. And I am briefing you about two incidents from the field of science:

1. When Charles Darwin proposed the 'Theory of evolution' and started to say that man had evolved from the apes, many people opposed the theory as it was against their religious ideologies and there was also a conspiracy to suppress this theory. But later, the truth came to light, shadowing the darkness. The world finally believed in Charles Darwin's theory of evolution which stated that man had evolved from the

apes and that every living organism on this planet had evolved from a single living organism.

2. In 1543, a scientist named Nicolaus Copernicus proposed a theory—'Copernican heliocentrism' which stated that the sun is near the center of the universe, motionless with the earth and the other planets revolving around it in a circular path, modified by epicycles and at uniform speeds, but this theory was against the beliefs of the medieval church. The medieval church believed in 'geo-centrism' which stated that the earth was at the center of the universe and the sun, moon and the other planets revolved around the earth in a circular path. Earlier, the theory of Nicolaus Copernicus was rejected by the medieval church and many people. Since the truth cannot be suppressed by the untruth for long, later the world and the medieval church believed in the 'Copernican heliocentrism' theory.

These two historic events from the field of science definitely throw some light on how the truth resurfaces and ultimately triumphs in the end.

Anything Can Fail In This World But Truth Will Never Fail.

Truth Alone Triumphs (Satyameva Jayathe)

In this book, the story starts at Brahma Muhurtham (dawn time), which is a very auspicious time according to the Hindus. According to the Hindus, this is the time which is most suitable to start any good activity for the day. But in this story, some municipal corporation (Govt. Dept.) people misuse their position for a wrong reason at Brahma Muhurtham. Let us see how.

Chapter 1

[The beginning, the very beginning of the story]

It was an early Monday morning around 4 am. The rain that had started around 9 pm on Sunday was yet mildly on, almost like a drizzle, which made the climate even colder than normal early mornings. In such a climate, any person whose activities begin as early as 4 am, will find it difficult to resist the climate's coldness and would want to continue their sound sleep for at least another two hours. Such was the chilliness in the air.

It is said that this time of the night we get a very sound sleep, and so no one wants to sacrifice their sleep for anything. But here, the people of Bangalore will be surprised to know that the municipal corporation people are awake and on duty at this time, who otherwise, usually stay away from their duties. The street-lights were off and it was a dark early morning. Two men in khaki are on a branch of a big tree, having axes in their hands and the other two men in khaki are standing below the tree, holding a rope that was tied to the branch of a tree, which the two men on the branch were about to cut. There was another man wearing a rain-coat, holding an umbrella, standing next to a Jeep and his name was Basavaraju. "Why have you not started cutting the branch of the tree?" shouted Basavaraju in a very high-pitched voice.

"It's too slippery and difficult to cut the branch with the axes," replied one of the men in khaki, in a painful tone.

"I know, that's the reason we are paid 3-months' salary for two hours by the mall people. Now, somehow start cutting the branch," replied Basavaraju in a contempt manner.

"You will anyway be safe standing near the Jeep, we are the ones who face the risk," murmured one of the khaki men on the tree, to himself. The two men adjusted their sitting positions and started cutting that big branch of the tree.

After a while...

"Fast, hurry up, we only have a little time left before anyone comes to know or before that idiot arrives," shouted Basavaraju.

The workers on the tree again murmured to themselves, and began cutting the branch faster. As the branch is cut to $3/4^{th}$ of its diameter, Basavaraju rushes towards the tree.

"Enough, you fools, it's enough. Now, stamp the branch down," shouted Basavaraju in a tensed voice and then shouted at the workers standing below the tree, "You two! Pull the rope with all your strength, and it will break and fall."

The two workers, who were cutting the branch, stopped cutting and started to stamp on the branch with their legs, each holding a branch for support. The two workers below applied all their strength to pull down the branch. Suddenly, the street-lights get lit and the roaring sound of the auto rickshaw engines reaches the municipality workers. Before they could react to the sound, a couple of auto rickshaw drivers rush towards the tree. Seeing the auto rickshaw, the two workers who were pulling the rope, drop the rope and start to run away. Couple of men from auto rickshaws get down and chase them. Five men get down from the two auto rickshaws and demand the two workers to get down from the tree. Among the five men, one man had an interesting look and his name was Basha.

He was a rather tall man, with a straight nose with a small scar in the middle. He had a firm mouth, dark complexion, very stylish hair, well-trimmed moustache, twinkling, sharp eyes and he had the look of a lion-hearted guy and a courageous man with leadership qualities.

Behind him were four of his trusted loyal friends. Two of the men had a well-built physique and a huge masculine body; the third one was a tall Sikh with a huge body, who wore a turban on his head and had an unshaved beard. The last one was a tall lean man with a clean-shaven face, and he looked like the right hand of Basha. He was clearly talented and a great guiding man for Basha.

All these four men were positioned as though they were guarding Basha and were waiting to take orders from him.

Couple of auto rickshaw drivers returned saying that the two workers ran away.

"Why are you cutting down the tree?" Basha questioned the workers, disapprovingly.

"We are from the municipal corporation and we have the right to cut down the tree," argued Basavaraju stubbornly.

Suddenly, a loud police-siren is heard, and within a minute, a couple of police constables and S.I. (Sub-Inspector) Ratnakar reach the spot and start questioning both the parties. S.I. Ratnakar was a short man in his fifties, with a dark-medium complexion with a huge pot belly, having small shoulders with big firm moustache and an exhausted look.

"What's going on here?" questioned the S.I. in a commanding tone.

"They have no right to cut down this tree or any of its branches," protested Basha in a raging voice.

"I have the stay order from court and they are violating the court order," said Basha.

"Calm down... calm down... let's talk about this in the police station," S.I. Ratnakar said, trying to calm down the situation.

"Please ask the two workers to come down from the tree," Basha said to the S. I. in an arguable tone.

"Hey, climb down from the tree," ordered the S.I., signaling to the workers.

Within seconds, the two workers got down from the tree and started walking towards the police Jeep along with Basavaraju.

"Everything was going smoothly," murmured Basavaraju to his workers in a very soft voice, "if you would have stamped the branch harder, it would have fallen earlier."

"Sir, we stamped the branch with all our strength," argued the fellow worker in a low voice, "even then the branch didn't break. I think the branch will fall shortly."

Basha, standing below the tree in the mild rain, was looking at the branch that they had almost chopped. Tears flowed down his eyes, but his tears were not visible due to the rain, which washed away the tears. Then his colleagues consoled Basha and slowly walked towards the auto rickshaw and headed to the police station.

Chapter 2

[The beginning of the end of this story]

It was Tuesday evening, around 5 pm. The climate was quite different from that of Monday morning, and it was a bright dusky evening, the sun hadn't yet turned yellowish-orange. Two men were coming out of an MNC office wearing formals, carrying a laptop bag and having a conversation of their own.

One of them was Basha's brother, Shashi Kumar. He was a tall man, with a straight nose, fair complexion, soft skin, clean-shaven face with no moustache. His eyes had a tired and exhausted look. All in all, he was a handsome, white-collared working guy. Both men parted, saying goodbyes to each other. As Shashi walked downstairs to his MNC office entrance stairs, he took out his mobile casually from his shirt pocket and went through the mobile screen. The mobile was in a silent mode, so there were eight missed calls. Shashi switched the mobile to general mode and opened the missed call list. On the mobile screen, five new missed call lists appeared. Shashi slowly scrolled down, looking at the five new missed call numbers.

1. Blood bank (2) missed calls
2. Ajith Kumar, Bro-in-law (2) missed calls
3. Sampath Uncle (1) missed call
4. Home (2) missed calls
5. New number (1) missed call

Initially, Shashi calls home, but no one picks the mobile. Again, he tries and the response is the same.

"What might be the reason for Ajith calling me?" he questions himself.

Then, he decides to call Ajith. After three rings, Ajith finally picks up the call.

"Hello Ajith! What's the reason for calling me?" asked Shashi, in a puzzled voice.

"Why didn't you pick up the call earlier, when I called you?" asked Ajith, in a sobbing voice.

"Because of some unnecessary calls, I had kept my mobile in silent mode," replied Shashi. "So, that's the reason I didn't pick up your call earlier," Shashi said.

"Ok, so what's the reason for calling me, Ajith?" Shashi again questioned with curiosity.

"Come fast to the Modern Hospital," said Ajith emotionally in a crying voice.

"Are you crying, Ajith?"

"Is everyone alright?"

"What's the reason?"

"Even Sampath Uncle called me earlier."

"Is something wrong? Please tell me, Ajith," asked Shashi in a confused voice, asking question after question.

"First, you come to the Modern Hospital quickly, even Sampath Uncle is here," cried Ajith, disconnecting the call.

Shashi gets tensed, puts the mobile in his shirt pocket and catches an auto rickshaw immediately. Shashi, sitting in the auto rickshaw, questions himself and imagines various situations.

"Why are Ajith and Sampath Uncle in the hospital?"

"What might be the reason?"

"Why was Ajith crying?"

"Why is he asking me to come fast to the hospital?"

And finally, he prays to God that nothing serious should have happened to his family.

As he was thinking of the various questions, the auto rickshaw reaches Modern Hospital main gate. Shashi pays the fare to the auto rickshaw driver and rushes into the hospital with a hurried pace. As soon as he enters into the reception hall of the hospital, Ajith spots Shashi.

"Hi Uncle," cried Ajith, lifting his hand above his shoulder.

Shashi, looking at Ajith and his family members, who were gathered in the reception hall of the hospital, rushed towards them. Shashi's wife, who was sitting on the floor and crying with her palms on her forehead, rushed towards Shashi and hugged him tightly. She started crying bitterly and exclaimed, "Our child is no more."

Shashi was in a terrible shock, as he clutched his wife to his chest.

"What happened to Rohith?" cried Shashi.

There was an absolute silence, apart from the sobbing noise of Shashi's wife.

Looking at his family, he cried, "What happened? Will someone please say something?"

"A BMTC bus ran over Rohith," cried Ajith and continued to narrate in a painful voice.

"It was the mistake of the driver who was talking on his mobile, that's why the accident happened. Rohith is in the ICU and doctors are asking to deposit Rs. 5 lakhs within two hours for the operation of Rohith. They have to operate on his head to remove the blood clot inside his head; else it will be difficult to save Rohith."

Hearing these words from Ajith, Shashi couldn't control his emotions and started crying loudly.

"How can we manage to arrange Rs. 5 lakhs in just two hours?" cried Shashi and continued to say, "Even if we sell all our ornaments, we won't be able to arrange Rs. 5 lakhs." Hugging his wife firmly, Shashi continued to yell to himself.

"Who is going to help us?"

"Why is this happening to me? Oh! God, why is this happening to me? Knowingly, I haven't committed any sin in my life, Oh! God, why didn't you take the life of the bus driver? It was his mistake to talk on the mobile while driving. Why did you punish my innocent child and family? What was my fault?" he questioned and cursed God.

Seeing his uncontrollable sorrow, an elderly lady spoke up.

"Has anyone informed my son, Basha about the accident?" questioned Shashi's mother Parvathamma. She was a well-aged woman of sixty years, wore a cotton sari and a matching blouse. Her hands were trembling due to old-age, when she was speaking.

No one spoke up.

"Have you informed your husband, Savitha?" Parvathamma asked Basha's wife in a clueless manner.

"No mother, I thought someone might have already informed," answered Savitha politely.

Savitha was a young married woman of average height with black pearl-like eyes and a beautiful nose, with a fair complexion, long hair and wore a well printed fancy saree and a matching blouse.

"Ok then.... now please call my son, Basha," cried Parvathamma to Ajith.

"Ok mother," replied Ajith.

Shashi was in a grieving state yet.

"Why are you calling Basha, mother?" cried Shashi. "He himself is in debt and needs money to get back his auto rickshaw from the mortgage. That's the reason he is driving auto rickshaw on a daily basis. So, how can he help in arranging Rs. 5 lakhs?" questioned Shashi logically.

"As an uncle, it is his right to know about Rohith's accident," cried Parvathamma.

"You please call your Basha Uncle, Ajith," requested Parvathamma.

Ajith started to dial Basha's number.

Let us all see what made God punish the innocent Shashi Kumar.

Chapter 3

KARMA

Yesterday (Monday) morning at 7:30

It is morning in Shashi's middle-class house. A mobile phone rings on a wooden tea-table. Shashi's wife is preparing breakfast in the kitchen, his son Rohith is getting ready for school by arranging his books in his bag. Shashi walks out of the kitchen, wearing a sleeveless vest with a pant and a cotton towel around his neck, holding a cup of tea in his hand. He slowly walks towards the tea-table to pick the mobile that was ringing for a while now.

Shashi takes the mobile phone in his right hand, holding his tea in his left hand, looking at the mobile screen. 'Basha Brother' flashed on the screen. He picks up the call, in a very hesitating manner.

"Hello brother," said Basha, the voice sounded muffled as it was in the loudspeaker mode.

"Uhhh...hello brother," answered Shashi in a low voice.

Few seconds later.

"What's the reason for calling?" questioned Shashi.

"Have you had your coffee and breakfast?" questioned Basha, in a pleasant tone.

"Yeah, I am having tea right now," said Shashi, sitting on the sofa and placing the tea on the wooden table.

"Has Rohit got up?" asked Basha.

"Yeah, he is getting ready for school."

"Uhhh….why did you call me?" asked Shashi, in a frustrated voice.

"Nothing, I just need you to write a small letter on my behalf" requested Basha in a pleasing voice.

"Ok, are you at your home or at the police station?" questioned Shashi.

Shashi's wife, who was preparing breakfast in the kitchen, gave a curious gaze to Shashi.

"At my home, and how did you know, brother?" asked Basha in a puzzled tone.

"Somehow and by the way, why are you opposing the municipality people?" asked Shashi in frustrated voice.

"No, my brother," said Basha politely, "I am not opposing the municipality people, I am only opposing the cutting down of the harmless trees."

"Who are you to oppose? The tree is in the middle of the road and the municipality people have the right to cut down the tree. If it was on your land, then the reason for your opposing would have been fair enough," argued Shashi in an irritated voice.

"It's not the matter of the tree being on our land or on the government property," argued Basha. "You know that the tree was planted by our grandparents and we have spent our childhood days under the tree. The only reason for cutting down that tree is because it is blocking the view of the shopping mall and the municipality officials are in favor of the shopping mall."

"Ok you win, it's useless talking to people like you," said Shashi. "What's the matter to be written, anyway?"

Basha said, "I just need you to write a letter against A.E. Basavaraju to the municipal corporation commissioner. Even though there is a stay order on cutting down of the tree, he is ignoring the stay order and attempting to cut it down. A severe legal action must be taken against them by the commissioner."

Shashi's wife came out of the kitchen, wiping the sweat from her forehead with her saree-end. She was an average Indian woman, with fair complexion, well curved nose, sharp eyes, exotic lips and with long black hair. Altogether, she was a beautiful house wife.

"My dear, the tea has gone cold, should I reheat it for you?" asked Shashi's wife, Rekha.

"Yeah, please do, my dear," requested Shashi. Rekha takes the tea cup into the kitchen to reheat it.

"Why are you wasting your time and money for the trees?" suggested Shashi in an arguing voice.

"My brother! Trees are very useful for mankind. They provide us with many useful things without expecting anything from us. But we, instead of protecting them, are cutting down the trees as if they are our enemies. Even then, they stand firm without complaining. We, being the dominant species of the planet, it is our duty to protect and preserve nature."

"Ok...ok, you preserve and protect nature, but I have no time to talk," replied Shashi.

There was a pause for a few seconds in the conversation.

Then Shashi said, "I will write the letter on your behalf, but I won't be available at the house, so come and collect the letter from my wife. Ok, bye."

"Thank you, my brother," said Basha politely.

Shashi cuts the call.

Shashi's wife serves the re-heated tea to Shashi.

"First of all, he himself is in a problem," said Shashi, with a teasing smile on his face. "Someone has to help him, and he is protecting some useless tree."

Rekha, who was standing next to him, said, "What your brother is fighting for is a good cause."

Shashi replied with a slight laugh, "Then you also support him for no good reason."

"My dear, I mean the tree was planted by your grandparents," explained Rekha.

"Everyone in that area used to worship the tree, and the municipal corporation people have no reason to cut down the tree, except those mall people. Being educated, we should help your brother," explained Rekha in a pleasing tone.

"If I start protecting trees like my brother, who will help run our family?" argued Shashi teasingly. "It is useless arguing with people like you and my brother. It's getting late for my office."

Sensing there is no need for further argument, Rekha paused for a few seconds.

Shashi, after finishing his tea, took out the book-pad from below the tea-table, which was meant for books, and started writing the letter. Rekha took the tea cup inside the kitchen.

After writing the letter, Shashi asked his wife to hand it over to Basha when he arrived. He also told her to ask him about having breakfast. In a few minutes, Shashi took his shower, had breakfast and got dressed for office.

Few minutes later, Shashi and his son Rohith left the house.

"Bye, my dear," said Shashi. "Bye mummy," said Rohith, waving his right hand.

"Empty the lunch box," Rekha said aloud.

Rain had now stopped, it was a beautiful clear day filled with bright morning sunlight.

Shashi's house was nearly one kilometer from the school. The only hurdle was the main road, through which Rohith had to go to school every day. The main road was connected to the city market, so usually the road would always be busy with city buses, auto rickshaws, two-wheelers and pedestrians.

After a while, Shashi left his son near the school gate, giving him Rs. 10 to have ice cream on his way back from the school. Then Shashi walked towards the bus stand. There was a very small *paan-shop* about thirty feet from the bus stand. The *paan-shop* was made of some kind of iron sheet with an area of six by four feet, and a single man could barely stand or sit in it. The shop was well decorated with plastic flowers on the outside and inside. The *paan-wala* was standing in the middle of the shop, cutting the betel-nuts into small pieces. Inside the shop, a variety of cigarettes and pan-masala packets were arranged neatly in the stands. A bunch of well-ripened bananas were hanging from the roof of the shop. The *paan-wala* was cutting the betel-nuts and preserving them in the stainless steel containers. There were a lot of steel containers, containing various ingredients of pan-masala, on a wooden show-stand in front of the shop. Also, there were two big black thermos flasks containing tea and coffee. Shashi reached the *paan-shop* and said "Bhai, one tea and a small one."(Small is a category of a brand of cigarettes, which is popular among middle-class people in India)

The *paan-wala* poured the tea into a plastic cup and picked a small cigarette from a packet and handed them over to Shashi. Shashi takes the tea and has a sip of it, for taste. He then lights his cigarette from the burning rope, (a by-product of coconut) which was tied at one end and had fire on the other. As usual, Shashi took a sip of tea and then a puff of the cigarette and continued the cycle till he finished the cigarette and the tea. He paid twenty rupees and then asked for a banana.

"Please pluck one, Sir," requested the *paan-wala*, who was busy cutting the betel-nuts.

Shashi plucked a banana and started to peel the skin of the banana. Slowly, he walked towards the bus stand. The bus stand was well designed, having all the amenities like a couple of chairs for the passengers to sit, a shelter-roof, a stainless steel grill for the safety of passengers and a dustbin which said- USE ME, KEEP THE CITY CLEAN. After finishing the banana, Shashi threw the banana peel on the footpath, walked to the bus stand and stood next to the dustbin, which was nearly twenty feet from the banana peel he had thrown. Being an educated citizen, it was his social responsibility to keep the city clean by using the dustbin. It was the bus stand where Shashi regularly waited for the buses, and he very well knew that there was a dustbin near the bus stand, but yet, he did not bother to use it to keep the city clean. After a while, he got into the bus and went to his office.

Many pedestrians who walked on the footpath also didn't bother to drop the banana peel into the dustbin. As it had rained last night, the footpath was slippery. On top of it, there was this banana peel which made the footpath a bit dangerous, for the pedestrians to walk.

Chapter 4

"Kiran, today is a very auspicious day," said Arvind, who was driving an imported SUV. Arvind was a big well-built man with scanty hair, a small broad nose, closely set eyes and a broad neck. He had well-built muscular arms, and wore a branded T-shirt and jeans.

"Why do you say that today is a very auspicious day?" asked Praveen, who was sitting next to Arvind, in the front seat of the SUV. Praveen was an average man, having a well-shaped body that fit into any kind of dress. He had thick black hair, piercing brown eyes, a fair skin tone, a narrow moustache and a sharp straight nose. Overall, he was a handsome and well-dressed twenty-eight years old man.

"Today, Kiran and Shwetha are getting married," Arvind replied in a joyous tone. "And the same evening, you are going to the United States for your beloved project," Arvind said teasingly.

Kiran, Shwetha and Revathi were sitting behind in the second row of the SUV. Kiran, being the groom, was wearing a navy-blue pant with an inserted creamy-white shirt and had spectacles for his bold eyes. He was a handsome man with a wheatish skin tone, above average personality, a big stomach, and weighed nearly eighty kilograms. Being the bride, Shwetha was sitting next to Kiran. She was wearing a maroon Kanchipuram silk saree with a matching silk blouse. She had long black hair, sparkling brown eyes, a beautiful small nose, small firm mouth, pink lips, with a bundle of jasmine flowers at the back of her head, her long hands were adorned with dozens of green glass-bangles. Being a bride in India, it's traditional to wear a silk saree, bangles and jasmine flowers.

"Yes, you are right, Arvind," said Revathi in a soft voice. Revathi gave Praveen a romantic look through the rearview mirror of the SUV. Revathi was a beautiful young woman, with short and silky dark hair, beautiful nose, shiny lips, round face, slim body, wearing a green silk saree with a matching blouse, a bundle of jasmine flowers at the back of her head, dozens of green bangles on both her hands. Altogether, she was a gorgeous woman with a fair skin tone. Her fair complexion was such that the greenish-looking blood veins were visible on her neck.

"Yeah, from our friends circle, Praveen will be the first person to go abroad for his dream project. If he gets the project, it might open up many job opportunities for other Indians," said Revathi excitedly.

Revathi and Praveen were both in love with each other, but both of them never expressed their feelings to each other. Even their friends knew about their love for each other. Suddenly, Revathi's mobile rings, and she takes out the mobile from her hand bag and picks up the call.

"Where are you, Revathi?" questioned Sneha in curiosity, from the other end of the call.

"I am at my friend's wedding," replied Revathi.

"Revathi, please don't miss the interview with the action star, Ranjith Kumar at around four o' clock tomorrow evening. And if it is not possible for you to do so, please inform me beforehand," requested Sneha in a suggestive tone.

"Sure…!" said Revathi. "Till today, has there been any interview that I have missed?"

"It's my duty to remind," argued Sneha politely.

There was a pause for a few seconds in the conversation.

"Ok, have a nice day. Bye," said Sneha.

"Thank you, Sneha. Bye." and the call ended.

"Whose call was that?" asked Praveen in curiosity.

"My program supervisor's," answered Revathi looking at Praveen through the rearview mirror of the SUV. "Revathi, is this about that program which used to capture the corrupt government officials through hidden cameras, that was later discontinued?" asked Praveen, looking at her in the rearview mirror.

"No, we didn't discontinue that candid corruption program, it was just that the person who was anchoring the program has gone to another TV channel," replied Revathi politely.

"Why don't you co-ordinate and anchor that program?" suggested Praveen encouragingly.

Suddenly, Revathi exclaimed in a surprise, "Oh! No, I don't have enough guts and courage to anchor." "Guts and courage are not in-born, they are cultivated according to situations," said Praveen.

"If you say so, then Revathi will sure anchor," teased Arvind with a little laughter.

"Me? No way," said Revathi.

"I would love to watch Revathi anchoring the show," encouraged Praveen in support. "The program used to help the poor people know about how things work in the government and it also helped to curb corruption in the government offices."

Hearing those words, Revathi's beautiful eyes melted in shyness, and started to look at Praveen's image through the front rearview mirror of the car with love and respect. Kiran, watching their romantic exchange of looks and knowing their affection and respect towards each other, teasingly said, "And by the way, I hope there will be another love marriage in our group."

"Yeah sure," said Arvind.

Praveen gave a soft tap on the shoulder of Arvind to stop teasing Revathi and him.

"Not until my dream project completes," said Praveen. Praveen smiled seeing Revathi in the rearview mirror. In a few minutes, the SUV reached the entrance of the temple.

The Kodanda Ramaswamy temple is one of the beautiful temples in the city. On either sides of the entrance of the temple, there are two beautifully carved granite statues of elephants, with the steps inclining upwards to the base of the Gopuram. The Gopuram was nearly fifty feet in height, with six bronze Kalashas on top of the Gopuram. It was a pleasant view to see the Gopuram from the top. The Gopuram itself was well designed and decorated with paint, and there were many characters and avatars of Lord Vishnu on the Gopuram. Inside the temple, we can find small and separate temples of Lord Ganesha, Lord, Hanuman and the main deity, Sri Kodanda Ramaswamy, which was straight opposite to the Gopuram entrance. Inside the chamber of Sri Kodanda Ramaswamy temple, there were statues of Sri Rama, Sita, Lakshmana and Hanuman.

Everyone from the car gets down. Revathi signals Praveen to bring along the gold chain, circling her hand around her neck animatedly. Praveen understood her sign and nodded affirmatively. "You people go inside the temple and make arrangements for the marriage. I will be there in a minute," requested Praveen.

"What's the reason?" questioned Kiran.

"Nothing…! You just go and make arrangements for the marriage," replied Praveen.

Then Revathi interrupted, "Come on Kiran, he will be back in a moment."

Kiran murmured to Arvind, "Nice understanding between you both, even before marriage." All four of them go inside the temple. In a few minutes, Praveen was at the jewelry shop, which was situated in the temple street. Praveen browsed through many kinds of gold chains which were displayed in the jewelry shop. After selecting one particular gold chain, Praveen asked the sales-boy to pack it for him. As the sales-boy was packing and billing the gold chain, Praveen's mobile rings. He picks up the call.

"Where are you? Come back fast," demanded Arvind. "The auspicious muhurtham is nearing, so please hurry up."

"I will be there in a minute," replied Praveen and cut the call.

"Please pack and bill the gold chain. I am in a hurry," requested Praveen to the cashier. After packing and billing the amount, the cashier said, "Sir, It's Rs. 80,000 for the forty grams of gold chain."

Praveen pays the amount for the gold chain, receives the payment slip and rushes towards the temple holding the gold-chain gift box in his hand. After a while, Revathi asked Arvind, "Have you made a call to Praveen? The auspicious time is running out."

"Yeah….! I had called him and he said that he will be here in a minute," replied Arvind.

Revathi was looking at Kiran and Shwetha, who were holding garlands in their hands, and the temple priest was performing pooja for the *mangalsutra*, in the deity's chamber.

According to the Hindu traditions, *mangalasutra* is a sacred thread made of turmeric paste and cotton thread with a piece of turmeric root tied at the center of the thread. This thread is tied to the bride, by the groom in the auspicious muhurtham (time). As soon as the *mangalasutra* is tied with 3 knots to the bride's neck, the bride becomes the wife of the groom, in the presence of God and with the witness of fire, water air, earth and space There is also a reason for tying the sacred thread to the bride's neck, i.e., when a man looks at a strange woman for the first time, his first sight goes towards her chest and then her face and body. So, when a man sees the married woman's chest with the hanging *mangalasutra*, his desire for her changes to a pure one because he can see that she is a married woman and looking at a married woman is considered a sin in all the religions. This becomes a symbol for the woman that she is married. And this *mangalasutra* is worn till the death of her husband.

Frustrated, Revathi looks at her wrist watch, takes out her mobile phone and calls Praveen. For a few seconds, the mobile rings and Praveen doesn't respond to her call. Frustrated, Revathi calls again. After a few rings, someone picks up the call on the other side.

"Hello Praveen, where are you?" asked Revathi in curiosity. From the other side of the call, a male voice asks, "Hello madam, are you Revathi?" The voice was kind of muffled as the crowd was murmuring in the distance.

"Yes. But, who are you?" enquired Revathi, all puzzled and confused with a bit of fear.

"My name is Vinu. Does this mobile phone belong to your friend?" asked Vinu politely.

"Yes, that is my friend Praveen's mobile phone," replied Revathi.

"Sorry to inform you, but your friend is injured and unconscious here. Also, there is heavy bleeding from his head," explained Vinu.

"What? Where? How?" cried Revathi in a disastrous shock.

"Near Kodanda Ramaswamy temple bus stand," said Vinu.

"We will be there in a minute," cried Revathi. She couldn't control her emotions and tears flowed from both the eyes. Aravind, Kiran and Shwetha were all shell shocked and asked if something was wrong. "Praveen is unconscious near the bus stand," Revathi cried deeply, wiping her eyes.

All the four friends were crying out of shock, as they rushed out of the temple, leaving the marriage to a halt. In a few seconds, they were outside the temple and proceeded on their left towards the bus stop. On their left, was a huge crowd gathered at a spot. Seeing the crowd, all the four friends rushed to the spot. Revathi and Shwetha, who were both crying, had to keep up with Aravind and Kiran, who were running towards the bus stop. As soon as they bisected the crowd and saw Praveen lying in a pool of blood, all the four friends fell to their knees. Shwetha helped Revathi place Praveen's head onto her lap, while Kiran and Aravind took Praveen's palms and started to rub on it.

"Poor fellow, stepped on a banana peel, while he was running towards the temple," said someone in the crowd.

The same banana peel which was thrown next to the dustbin by the irresponsible and reckless Shashi.

"Please hurry up and take him to the hospital," suggested Vinu.

"Bring the car fast," Kiran cried to Arvind. Arvind leaves Praveen's hand and rushes to bring the car.

"Is there any hospital nearby?" cried Revathi.

"Yes, at the next cross, there is a corporation hospital," suggested Vinu.

In seconds, Arvind brought the car and jumped out of the driver's seat to open the passenger door. Along with Vinu, few other people helped Kiran, Revathi and Shwetha lift Praveen's unconscious body. After they were seated in the car, Revathi took Praveen's head on her lap. Vinu handed over Praveen's mobile to Revathi.

"Thanks for helping out," cried Kiran and Revathi. "It's all right, now go fast to the hospital," Vinu suggested.

The SUV headed towards, the corporation hospital in a furious way.

Few minutes later, they were near the main gate of the corporation hospital.

As soon as the car reached the entrance of the hospital, Kiran jumped out of the car to bring the stretcher. As Kiran came pushing the stretcher, Revathi, Arvind and Shwetha were ready to shift their unconscious friend onto the stretcher. After shifting him onto the stretcher, they rushed the stretcher inside the hospital.

It was an old unpainted corporation hospital. Looking at the hospital from the outside, anyone could judge the interiors of the hospital.

There was no painting on the weak infrastructure of the hospital, except for the rain patches and the broken windows all over. Even the name board of the hospital was washed over by the rain. Because of the lack of maintenance, the building structure was depreciating very quickly.

The interiors of the hospital were a nightmare for the rich and foreign visitors as this sight was similar to that of hell. At the entrance of the hospital was a reception cabin, behind which there was a board displaying the doctor's name, education and their services. Next to that, there was a narrow chamber indicating casualty. There was dirt all over the casualty floor. In the casualty chamber, there were three wooden tables, which were full of patients. Some patients were standing and the remaining who could not stand, were lying or sleeping on the floor.

Seeing the empty receptionist cabin and the board displaying that the doctors were in, they rushed the stretcher into the casualty ward. As soon as they entered the casualty ward, an awful odor blew onto their faces. Due to the smelly blow, Shwetha instantly started to vomit. The awful smell was due to the burn-injury patients. Shwetha left the stretcher and bent over to vomit in the casualty ward itself. Kiran rushed towards Shwetha, asking her whether she was alright.

Leaving the stretcher behind, Arvind rushed into the doctor's cabin. To his surprise, there was no doctor in the cabin, instead there was a compounder and a nurse, who were having snacks.

"Please help my friend," shouted Arvind. The compounder, looking at Arvind's big built personality and branded T-shirt, slowly comes out of the cabin while whispering something to the nurse.

"These patients don't even allow us to have our snacks in peace," murmured the compounder to himself and the nurse.

By this moment, the poor patients have circled around the Praveen's stretcher, looking at the unconscious body in a very pitiful manner. Shwetha and Kiran walked towards the stretcher with discomfort.

Looking at Praveen, the compounder instantly said "Oh! He has got a serious head injury. To remove the blood clot in the head, he must be operated immediately."

"Please do whatever it takes but please save his life," cried Revathi, folding her hands firmly.

"To do the operation, doctor is required, and the doctor hasn't come yet," said the compounder.

"What? It's already noon and the doctor hasn't yet come?" shouted Arvind.

An old woman, around eighty-years old, with wrinkled skin all over her body said "Yes, my son, these merciless doctors have their own private clinics and only after attending their clinic patients, they come here and attend to us. No man has the courage to ask about this injustice and the cruelty towards the poor patients."

Pointing to her pregnant daughter, the old woman continued to vent her anger towards the hospital doctors and authorities.

"See, my pregnant daughter and I have been going from cabin to cabin for the last two days. These people have no mercy and do not even bother to ask what the problem is," cried the old woman, displaying her anger towards the hospital authorities.

"Stop shouting, you idiot!" shouted the compounder to the old woman, in a disrespectful manner.

"It's better to take this boy to National Private Hospital which is in the next cross itself," suggested the old lady.

"Yeah! It's better to take Praveen to National Private Hospital instead of wasting our time here by arguing pointlessly," said Kiran.

They then rushed the unconscious body back to the SUV and then to the National Private Hospital. The National Private Hospital was one of the biggest private hospitals in the city. It was a five-storied building with a parking space for cars and two-wheelers. The reception hall itself was nearly 10,000 square feet, with a couple of women staff wearing a uniform saree, were standing at the entrance to help the out-patients. The floor of the reception hall was clean and shiny with a pleasant fragrance.

As soon as the car reached the entrance of the hospital, a couple of attenders who were standing with the stretcher, rushed towards the car and carried the unconscious Praveen on the stretcher and into the emergency ward.

All the four friends were stopped at the entrance of the emergency ward by a security guard. After a few minutes, a doctor and nurse came out of the emergency ward with some papers and walked towards the four friends.

"Are you the friends of the unconscious young man with the head injury?" asked the doctor.

The doctor was a young man, with coal-black hair, a straight nose and he sported a narrow moustache. He looked like in his thirties.

"Yes!" answered all the four friends simultaneously.

"He is in a serious condition and an operation has to be done to remove the blood clotting in his brain," explained the doctor.

"You may do any operation, but first, please try to save Praveen," cried Revathi.

"Then you have to deposit Rs. 5,00,000 in advance," said the doctor.

"Ok doctor, we will deposit the money in a few moments," cried Kiran, taking out the credit card from his wallet.

Then the doctor advised the nurse to help the four friends fill some formality papers and pay the advance bill. After paying the bill, Shwetha insisted on informing Praveen's parents about the accident, so Revathi called and informed them about the accident.

Nurses took the unconscious body inside the operation theatre. After a while, the nurses came out of Operation Theatre (OT) and asked Revathi to collect the belongings of the patient.

Revathi went inside the operation theatre and collected Praveen's wrist watch, ring, wallet and a purchased receipt of the gold chain from his shirt pocket. Then she realized that someone in the crowed had stolen the gold chain from the unconscious Praveen.

In a few minutes, Praveen's father and mother reached the hospital.

After a couple of hours, the surgeons came out of the operation theatre. The surgeon was a short man, with a small bald head, a straight nose, firm mouth and piercing eyes, wearing a doctor's typical white coat with a name tag—R.R. Singh. Revathi rushed towards the surgeon.

"The operation is successful, but he has to be in the ICU for two to three days. If he was brought here a little earlier, then there would not have been such complications in the blood clotting. After a few minutes, all of you can see him in the ICU, but don't disturb the patient," saying this, the doctor walked out.

After a while, Praveen was shifted to the ICU from the post-operation ward. The ICU was a well isolated cabin with a glass door that was being fixed. Through the glass door, the visitors could see the patients. All the four friends and Praveen's parents were looking at Praveen and they started crying, holding each other's hands. It was impossible to console them as they were emotionally devastated at that time.

After seeing Praveen for few minutes, they all returned to the waiting hall and sat on a narrow table. Revathi, who was sitting next to Praveen's parents, could not control her emotions and was crying bitterly. Suddenly, Praveen's mobile phone, which was with Revathi, rings. She attends the call.

"Hi Praveen, you must be here by 22nd evening for the meeting. So, you better leave India today itself," said Ramesh in a jolly mood.

"Hello, sorry Sir, may I know who is speaking?" asked Revathi.

"I am Ramesh from the US. May I know who is this?" asked Ramesh, a bit confused.

"I am Praveen's friend, Revathi," cried Revathi.

"Where is Praveen?" enquired Ramesh, quite puzzled by now.

"Sorry to say, but Praveen just met with an accident and he is in the ICU," cried Revathi.

"That's impossible. What are you saying? I have just spoken with him in the morning. He must be in the US by 22nd evening, else he will lose the clients to the other company.

Please tell him to attend the meeting or he is going to lose his dream project," Ramesh explained clearly to Revathi.

"OK, the accident happed at noon and I will inform him about this," replied Revathi.

"Sorry to hear that Praveen met with an accident and please don't forget because this is his dream project, through which many job opportunities will be created in the Indian company," requested Ramesh.

"Ok, thank you," cried Revathi.

"Thank you," said Ramesh. Then, Revathi cuts the call.

After a while, Revathi closes her eyes and begins thinking about Kiran and Shwetha's halted marriage, Praveen's dream project, Praveen's parents and the gold chain, and slowly falls into a slumber.

In her dream, she hears the voice of the old lady in the corporation hospital.

"No man has the courage to ask about this injustice and the cruelty towards the poor patients."

She then begins hearing the voice of the doctor.

"If he was brought here a little earlier...."

Scenes of the gold chain getting stolen and the halted marriage of Kiran and Shwetha kept hurling in Revathi's inner mind.

Another voice echoed in her dream.

"I would love to watch Revathi anchor the show; the program used to help the poor people understand the workings of the government and also help curb the corruption among the government officials."

The next morning around eight o' clock, she was being woken up by Dr. R.R. Singh.

"Praveen's condition is improving," said the doctor. "And there is no need to wait here, if there is any emergency, we will call you." The other members also woke up, as the doctor walks out of waiting room. Revathi walks into the rest room, washes her face and comes out.

"I have some unfinished business to do. I will return around 2 pm," said Revathi to her friends and Praveen's parents and walked out of the waiting room.

Then, coming out of the hospital, Revathi takes out her mobile and calls the Program Head (Supervisor) of the candid corruption show and requests to grant her the permission to direct and anchor the show. The Program Head grants her the permission.

Then, Revathi calls Sneha and informs her that she will miss the interview with the action star—Ranjith Kumar and apologizes for the same. She then calls the camera-man and asks him to come to the corporation hospital.

Chapter 5

In a private clinic, a doctor named Yadav Pandey, who is seated in his chair. He is a tall fifty-year old, with broad shoulders, black hair with a few white strands, bolted nose, brown eyes and with a wheatish complexion.

The private clinic of Dr. Yadav Pandey was divided into four cabins, one cabin was for the doctor to examine the patients, the second cabin was for the patients to wait, in the third cabin, some lab apparatus were present and the same room used as patients resting room and the fourth cabin was for the pharmacy. Each cabin was divided from the other by an aluminum fabrication.

In the doctor's cabin, there was immovable stretcher-cum-bed where the patients were examined, and a LCD television set was mounted on the wall opposite to the doctor's chair and table. On the doctor's table, there were some medicine bottles, packets of tablets, capsules, stethoscope and the doctor's name plate stating Doctor Yadav Pandey, MBBS FRC, Foreign Return Chief of Corporation Hospital. In the patient's waiting room, there were rows of tables for the patients to sit and wait. In the patient's resting room there were four beds with patients resting on them and in the pharmacy, there was a teenager boy who gave medicines according to the doctor's prescription.

A mobile phone rings on the table of Dr. Yadav Pandey. He picks up the call saying "Dr. Yadav Pandey here." On the other side is Dr. Chandra Mouli, who is a friend of Dr. Yadav Pandey.

"Hello doctor, I am Dr. Chandra Mouli."

"How are you?"

"I am fine."

"Why did you call me?" asked Yadav.

"Oh! You yet don't know the reason," teased Chandra Mouli.

"What reason?" asked Yadav.

"Switch on the TV and watch the QTV news channel," said Chandra Mouli.

"Why, what's going on, on the channel?" asked Yadav.

"What happened in the morning?" asked Chandra Mouli.

"Ohhh......... nothing!" replied Yadav.

"Ohh nothing, nothing? You will come to know, you first switch on the TV," said Chandra Mouli.

Yadav Pandey rings the call-bell on his table. A nurse comes inside the doctor's chamber.

"Please switch on the TV," said Yadav to the nurse.

Nurse switches the TV on and hands over the remote to the doctor.

Dr. Yadav Pandey anxiously presses the buttons on the remote and halts at QTV channel.

The candid corruption program of Revathi with Dr. Yadav Pandey was being telecasted on the TV.

On the TV screen, Revathi was holding the mic in her hand and introducing the program.

"I am Revathi, reporting to the QTV news channel for the program "Candid Corruption."

"Hello audience, today in our program you're going to watch a chief doctor of corporation hospital,

who runs his private clinic in his house and after attending his clinic patients, he visits the corporation hospital around 2 'o' clock, where he works as a Head of Department (HOD)."

"Come on, let's meet Dr. Yadav Pandey around 11 'o' clock at his home-cum-clinic, giving treatment to his patients."

The channel then shows the whole sting operation in detail.

Revathi enters the clinic. The hidden camera which is mounted on her dress shows the wall-clock and the nurse calling the patient's token number.

Revathi takes the token number from the nurse.

After a couple of patients, the nurse calls Revathi's token number. Again the hidden camera shows the time which is now 11:45 am. Revathi enters the cabin of the Dr. Yadav Pandey.

As she enters the doctor's cabin, Yadav Pandey has a thorough look at Revathi and her chest.

"Please take your seat," said Dr. Yadav Pandey.

Revathi sits on the chair, saying "Thank you, doctor."

Yadav Pandey again looks at her face and her chest for a while and gives a couple of heavy breaths.

"What is your problem?" asked Dr. Yadav Pandey.

Revathi said "Doctor, my name is Revathi. I am a software engineer by profession. I got a job in the US and so I need a medical certificate from a certified doctor stating that I am not a HIV +ve patient, and that I do not have any STD and also that I am medically fit to work in a foreign company. So, I first went to the corporation hospital. There, the compounder informed me that the chief doctor, that is you, will be available at your home-cum-clinic. So, here I am."

"Okay… so you just need a medical certificate and nothing else, right? asked Dr. Yadav Pandey.

"Yes, absolutely," replied Revathi.

"First, you have to take the HIV test, some blood tests and urine tests and after seeing the reports, I will give you the certificates," explained Dr. Yadav Pandey.

"Doctor, I am in a hurry. I need the certificates without any new tests and I have some four-year old medical report. Referring these reports, you could make the new reports," requested Revathi.

"Ok……then it will cost you more," said Dr. Yadav Pandey.

"It's Ok doctor, how much?" asked Revathi.

"Around Rs. 5000," answered Dr. Yadav Pandey.

"It's okay doctor," said Revathi.

Dr. Yadav Pandey rings the call-bell. A nurse comes inside the cabin.

"Prepare the complete HIV report, urine and blood test report for this lady," commanded Yadav Pandey to the nurse, pointing to Revathi.

"Reports with test or without?" questioned the nurse casually.

"Report without test, referring her four-year old report, prepare a new report," replied Dr. Yadav Pandey.

"Come with me," said the nurse to Revathi.

Revathi and the nurse go out of the cabin.

Dr. Yadav Pandey glanced at Revathi's back-side, as if measuring every inch of her body.

Nurse sits in her chair and questions Revathi about her age, present address and contact number.

Revathi replies to all her questions.

The nurse takes out the old reports of Revathi and starts preparing the new report.

Finally, after typing the report, the nurse asks to pay the amount.

Revathi pays Rs. 5000/- and takes the receipt.

Revathi and the nurse, along with new reports enter Dr. Yadav Pandey's cabin.

"Doctor, the report is ready," said the nurse,

"Has she paid the bill?" asked Dr. Yadav Pandey.

"Yes, doctor," answered the nurse.

"How much?" asked Yadav Pandey.

"Rs. 5000," replied the nurse.

"Ok, give the report and wait outside," commanded Dr. Yadav Pandey to the nurse.

Revathi walks to the chair and sits in the chair. Dr. Yadav Pandey goes through the report.

"Doctor till what time will you be in the clinic?" questioned Revathi.

"Till 2 pm," replied Dr. Yadav Pandey.

"If you need, I will meet you outside the clinic too," replied Dr. Yadav Pandey in an alluring voice.

"Where doctor?" asked Revathi.

"In a hotel or a park," replied Dr. Yadav Pandey.

"I mean, when will you be in the corporation hospital?" asked Revathi.

"I can't say exactly, but around 2 to 3 pm, I will be in the hospital."

"You can also meet me there," suggested Dr. Yadav Pandey.

Suddenly in a normal voice, without hesitation, he asks "Uhh....what is your bra size?"

"Excuse me, doctor?" asked Revathi in utter shock. The question hit her like a lightning bolt.

"What's your bra size?" asked Dr. Yadav Pandey, very shamelessly.

"Is this necessary, doctor? Is it for the report?" asked Revathi in an uncomfortable manner.

"No, but it is essential for the doctor," explained Dr. Yadav Pandey, very calmly.

"Thirty-four," replied Revathi.

"Fine," says the doctor and breathes in and out heavily.

Dr. Yadav Pandey signs and seals the report.

Revathi takes the report and gets up from the chair.

"Hello Miss. Revathi, if you need anything you can contact me," said Dr. Yadav Pandey, handing over his visiting card.

"Excuse me?" asked Revathi shockingly.

"I mean, any report in future," replied Dr. Yadav Pandey.

Revathi walks out of the cabin without saying a 'thanks' to the doctor.

Now, Yadav Pandey's eyes move away from the television screen.

Suddenly a mobile phone rings.

Yadav Pandey picks up the phone.

On the other side was a nurse named Kamala, from the corporation hospital.

"Doctor, it's an emergency, please come to the hospital immediately," said Kamala in a struggling tone.

"What bloody emergency has come up in the hospital?" shouted Yadav Pandey in anger.

"Sorry to say doctor, some media persons are demanding to see our attendance register and also our medical pharmacy account books," explained Kamala.

"It would be better if you come to the hospital before anything goes wrong."

"You idiot, don't allow anyone to show the pharmacy account books to anyone. I will be there in a minute," said Yadav Pandey. He cuts the call and then searches for a number in his mobile and dials the found number.

"Hello Inspector Karim, I am Dr. Yadav Pandey. Please come to our corporation hospital," requested Yadav Pandey, in a hurried voice.

"What's the problem, doctor?" asked Inspector Karim.

"Please come Sir, it's an emergency," requested Yadav Pandey.

"Ok, doctor," replied Inspector Karim and cut the call.

Dr. Yadav Pandey rings the call-bell and the nurse comes in.

Dr. Yadav Pandey takes the car keys from the drawer and hurries to the hospital.

"Close the clinic and send all the patients," shouted Dr. Yadav Pandey to the nurse Mary.

Yadav Pandey gets out of his clinic, starts the car and speeds away in a hurry.

Nurse Mary sends all the remaining patients back home and comes to the doctor's cabin and watches the television, which was still running the program 'Candid Corruption.'

Mary's eyes grow big in surprise.

Revathi was near the car, outside the corporation hospital holding a mic in her hand.

"Hello audience, welcome back to the 'Candid Corruption' show. Just now you witnessed that Dr. Yadav Pandey give a fake certificate for Rs. 5000, and now we are standing outside the corporation hospital,

where Dr. Yadav Pandey works as a HOD."

"It's already 1 o' clock in the afternoon and yet the doctor hasn't come to the hospital. The poor patients are waiting for the doctor. Many patients are going to the private clinic. Let's enter the hospital and see the attendance register."

Revathi enters the hospital along with the camera-man and two assistants.

As soon as the attendant sees the media persons, he gets nervous and tries to call the doctor.

Then Revathi stops him and asks him to show the attendance register.

The attendant struggles to speak and hesitantly shows the attendance register. Then Revathi takes it by force and shows it to the camera.

"Now, you are seeing the attendance register of the corporation hospital," said Revathi.

The total number of nurses and attendants are eighteen and the numbers of the doctors are five. Among them, Dr. Yadav Pandey is the chief doctor. All the members' attendance are marked, but no doctors' are marked. And only five to six nurses are present. Come on now, let's see the pharmacy accounts books.

Then a nurse in one of the cabins calls Dr. Yadav Pandey.

"Hello doctor, it is an emergency, please come to the hospital immediately," said nurse Kamala to Dr. Yadav Pandey in a struggling voice.

"What bloody emergency has come up in the hospital?" shouted Dr. Yadav Pandey in anger.

"Sorry to say doctor, but some media persons are demanding to see our attendance register and our medical pharmacy account books. It would be better if you come to the hospital before anything goes wrong," said Kamala.

"You idiot, don't allow anyone to show the pharmacy account books to anyone, I will be there in a minute." Revathi continued to interview the poor patients in the hospital and nurse Mary switched off the television.

Chapter 6

Vinu, sitting on a bench behind a huge bush in a big park, was waiting for an important person to arrive.

The big park was divided into two halves; one side was a plain ground along with a jogger-track for jogging and walking and the other portion was meant for trees, plants and bushes along with stone slabbed benches all around the park.

These bushes were very useful for love couples because it was not easy for anybody to identify the person or their activities behind the bushes.

A perfectly seducing beautiful aunty walks into the park and sits on the stone-slab next to Vinu. Seeing her, Vinu gets immensely pleased.

"Come closer, my dear," Vinu pleaded to Swarna in loving tone.

Swarna was a tall woman, around thirty years old, with broad shoulders, big arms, long hair, small nose, beautiful lips, dimple chins, wheatish skin tone and she was wearing a pink saree and a matching blouse. Here saree was worn in a very erotic manner. She was a very seductive woman indeed.

"What difference does it make?" said Swarna harshly.

"Why are you so harsh, my dear?" asked Vinu in very pleasing voice and tried to hug her.

"First, tell me why did you call me here urgently?" asked Swarna very rashly, pushing him away to avoid his hug.

"Why are you harsh, my dear? I have a present for you," said Vinu softly.

"Oh! Is it the same old biryani? Or halwa?" asked Swarna.

"No my dear, this time it's a gold chain," answered Vinu, pulling out the gold chain from his top pocket.

"A gold chain?" shouted Swarna, in a pleasant surprise. She plucked the gold chain from Vinu's hand and asked "Is this really gold or just gold-plated?" asked Swarna, doubtingly.

"No my dear, it is pure 916 gold," explained Vinu, slowly hugging Swarna.

"How many grams is it?" asked Swarna.

Struggling to speak, Vinu said "It's 40 grams, my dear."

"This looks heavy, where did you get it?" asked Swarna.

"I have bought it for your lovely neck, my dear," said Vinu.

"How did you arrange the money for it? asked Swarna.

"Somehow I managed to buy it, that's none of your business. Now it's your turn to give me a treat as per your deal, my dear," said Vinu.

"If it is pure gold, I am surely going to give you your treat, my dear," said Swarna. She gets up and wears the chain on her neck.

"I think you are in a hurry," said Vinu.

"Yes, tomorrow you will come to know why I am in such a hurry," she said shyly.

"Please tell me now itself," pleaded Vinu shyly.

"I want to show this gold chain to my friends," said Swarna as she walked out of the park.

"These women are all the same. As soon as they get some new stuff, they want to show off," said Vinu to himself.

Swarna was walking alone wearing the gold chain on the outside of her blouse. She was showing off the gold chain on the road. Although there were very few people on the road to look at her and the gold chain, she was very proud of her beauty and the gold chain. As she was walking on the road, she sees a bike rider and a pillion, both wearing black jackets and having helmets in their hands. As she passes by them, both of them glance at her strongly and the pillion gets excited and delightfully says "Here is our goat (victim)."

Both the rider and pillion wear their helmets and start the bike. They follow her slowly and the pillion on the bike snatches the gold chain from her and gets away on the speeding bike. Shocked, Swarna starts to shout for help.

"Help! Help! Thieves! My chain! My gold chain! Please someone catch them! Please help me." A couple of people on the street turn and see her. The rider accelerates the bike even faster. One young man named Shiva, was with his friends on the streets.

He was a tall young man around twenty-five years old, with big shoulders, strong arms, well-built biceps and triceps, small head, piercing brown eyes, pointed nose and with a dark complexion.

Shiva starts running towards the thief and tries to catch the pillion.

The bike rider accelerates the vehicle to its maximum speed, but Shiva's athletic running speed is even faster and somehow he manages to catch the collar of the pillion thief. After getting a hold of the collar, Shiva tries to drag him out from the bike.

The bike rider realizes that his fellow pillion's collar has been caught and that a few people are chasing the bike. He deliberately drives towards the turning point. Even at the turning point, Shiva's strong hands firmly grip the collar of the pillion. Then suddenly, a speeding car misses the bike and hits Shiva at the turning point.

The force of the collision was such that Shiva is thrown nearly ten feet high and he lands on the road unconscious.

The two thieves get away with the gold chain. The people and Shiva's friend slowly surrounds the unconscious body of Shiva. Slowly, blood started to flow from all over Shiva's body. Shiva's friend helped him to get to the hospital.

The speeding car which crashed against Shiva was driven by Dr. Yadav Pandey, who was in a hurry to get to the corporation hospital to stop the 'Candid Corruption' program on the QTV news channel. Dr. Yadav Pandey did not even bother to stop and have a look at the accident; instead he zoomed away in the car.

In a few minutes, Shiva was admitted in the National Hospital and he was in the ICU. Shiva's mother and some of his friends were waiting in the reception room. Shiva's mother was a fifty years old poor women with wrinkled skin, dark complexion, small head, white hair and she wore an unwashed cotton printed saree and a blouse.

A doctor and nurse come out of the ICU. Seeing the doctor, Shiva's friend, Murali got up.

Murali was a tall young man around twenty-seven years of age, with broad shoulders, well-built physique, piercing hazel eyes, flat nose, with a wheatish skin tone. Overall, he was an upper middle-class young man.

"Who is the relative of the patient Shiva?" asked Dr. Santosh.

Murali and Shiva's mother, along with other friends rushed to the doctor.

"Doctor, she is Shiva's mother," Murali introduced her to the doctor.

"Shiva has got heavy head and leg injury, because of which there is a heavy loss of blood from his body, so Shiva needs O – ve (negative) blood group to compensate the blood lost. In our blood bank too, there is a shortage of O –ve blood. It is a very rare blood group. So if anyone with O -ve blood group is here, they may kindly donate some blood," explained Dr. Santosh,

Murali was murmuring to himself that his blood group is not O -ve.

"Take my blood as he is my only son;" cried Shiva's mother.

Doctor looks at Shiva's mother poor undernourished body.

"What's your age, Amma?" questioned the doctor.

"Around fifty years," answered Murali.

"No mother, we cannot take blood from you as you are underweight, even if it may be O -ve blood." Her shoulders begin to quiver with despair and hopelessness.

Murali knew that none of his friend or his blood is O -ve.

"Doctor, is there any other way to get O –ve blood?" asked Murali.

"Go to our blood bank and they might help you, don't waste your time standing here," suggested Dr. Santosh.

"Ok, doctor," said Murali and rushed towards the blood bank with a couple of his friends.

Shiva's mother sits on the table, along with a few friends.

Murali along with his friends rushed to the blood bank receptionist desk. At the blood bank reception desk was a pretty young woman named Sonia. She was a beautiful woman with loose hair, fair complexion, small nose, pink lips, beautiful ears with hanging earrings. Her well-designed saree and blouse enhanced her beauty even more.

Murali and his friends reached the blood bank reception desk.

"Dr. Santosh has sent us to see O -ve blood group," said Murali.

"Are you from the patient Shiva's side?" asked Sonia.

"Yes, Madam," replied Murali.

"There is a shortage of O -ve blood and it is also a very rare blood group," said Sonia.

"Is there are other way, Madam?" asked Murali.

"Usually, if there is any shortage of blood of any group, then we give advertisement in TV, newspaper and in cellular networks," explained Sonia.

"Since in your case it's an emergency, we have another option."

"What's the other option, Madam?" asked Murali.

"We have the phone numbers and addresses of the rare blood group donors. We could call or meet them directly and request them to donate blood," answered Sonia.

"Then please call the O -ve blood donors for help, Madam," requested Murali.

"In such cases, we have a small issue," said Sonia.

"What's the small issue?" asked Murali.

"We will call them, but it is up to you to convince them to donate, by offering some money or valuables."

"Ok…Madam," replied Murali.

Sonia opens the screen of the computer and types O -ve blood and searches for the list of donors. The screen opened, listing the name, address, mobile number, age, blood group, gender and the last date of blood donated.

In the list, the first name was Shashi Kumar, male, who last donated blood 24 months back as detected on the screen of the computer.

"Shashi Kumar is best suited because it's been two years since he donated any blood," suggested Sonia.

Sonia calls Shashi Kumar pressing the keypads of the land line. Shashi Kumar picks up the call.

Shashi was in his office. His office was nearly ten thousand square feet in space. This space was divided into small cabins with fiber-glass. One separate cabin was allotted to all the workers. In these cabins, a desktop, a chair and a land line connection was provided to each worker, similar to the office cabins of software companies or call centers.

"Hello Sir, is this Shashi Kumar?" asked Sonia.

"Yes, Madam," answered Shashi.

"My name is Sonia. I am calling from blood bank department of National Hospital. We have an emergency case in which we have a shortage of O -ve blood. So, we request you to donate some blood," said Sonia.

"Sorry Madam, I am in the office. I can't come now, so please try another blood donor, Madam," Shashi said.

"It's a matter of life and death," said Sonia, in a pleading tone.

"Sorry Madam," said Shashi and cut the call.

Shashi Kumar thinks to himself "Nonsense, am I the only one person with O -ve blood group?"

"Sorry, but he is not willing to donate," said Sonia.

"Please try again, Madam. Let me talk to him," requested Murali.

Sonia redials and hands the receiver to Murali.

Shashi Kumar picks up the call.

"Sorry Madam, I can't come right now," protested Shashi Kumar.

"Sir, my name is Murali, my friend is in need of O -ve blood. Please help him. He is the only one son to his mother. If you want, we can even give money for the blood," cried Murali.

"Sorry, I can't come right now," said Shashi. "I have already donated my blood three months ago and again I can't donate now."

"Sir, after every forty-five days, a healthy person can donate blood," explained Murali.

"If I do donate, I might get some blood related diseases," said Shashi.

"Nothing will happen, Sir. You will be perfectly alright," Murali pleaded.

"Sorry Sir, I am busy now," said Shashi and disconnected the call in anger.

A man named Karan Saxena rushed to Sonia's desk asking where Adithya, an acid attack victim was admitted?

"This is a blood bank reception desk. Sir, please ask in the main reception," said Sonia and gave him the directions to the main reception hall.

Murali said, "Please redial the number again, Madam."

Shashi, on the other side, switches his mobile to silent mode.

Murali redials but Shashi doesn't pick up the mobile. Again Murali redials, but he doesn't pick up the mobile as it is in a silent mode.

Sonia suggested, "Let's try another donor."

Sonia points the cursor to the second name on the screen. The name appears as Damodar. Sonia calls Damodar, pressing the keypad of the land line. Damodar was driving a crowded BMTC bus in the busy Bangalore streets. It was an offence and a mistake to attend a mobile call during driving a bus. But even then, Damodar attended the call.

"Hello Sir, is this Damodar?" asked Sonia.

"Yes Madam, who are you?" asked Damodar.

"My name is Sonia and I am calling from blood bank department of National Hospital."

"Fine....What's the reason for calling me?" asked Damodar.

"We have an emergency case in which we have a shortage of O -ve blood, so we request you to come here and donate some blood," said Sonia.

"Ok Madam, but I am a BMTC bus driver having one more trip. After completing that, I will come to your hospital to donate blood," said Damodar.

"Please Sir, make it fast," requested Sonia.

In a fraction of a second, as he was speaking on the mobile, he loses his concentration on the road and is unable to control the steering. The bus is now on the foot path.

Striking a tree and finally with a school-child, who was walking alone, having an ice cream in his hand.

The frightened Damodar, without cutting the call, puts the mobile in his upper pocket and runs away, leaving the bus. The people on the streets and the passengers in the bus rush to see the child. "Oh! my God, this is the fault of the bus driver as he was talking on the mobile," said a man in the bus.

"Where is he?" asked another man.

"He ran away. The tree reduced the speed of the bus, otherwise there would have been more victims apart from this child."

Someone with a good heart stopped an auto rickshaw. A couple of people help the man lift the child, to admit him in the hospital. On the child's identity-card the name was Rohith, and father's name was Shashi Kumar. Some good men admitted the child to the Modern Hospital.

Chapter 7

As the readers of this story, we all now came to know the sin of Shashi Kumar. Let us continue the story.

"How can we manage to arrange Rs. 5 lakhs in just two hours?" cried Shashi and continued to say that even if they sold all their ornaments, they wouldn't be able to manage up to Rs. 5 lakhs.

Shashi started to shout and yell, "Who is going to help us? Why is this happening to me? Oh! God, why is this happening to me? Knowingly, I haven't committed any sin in my life."

"Oh! God, why didn't you take the life of the bus driver? It was his mistake to talk over the mobile phone while driving. Why did you punish my innocent child and family?"

"What was my fault?" he questioned and cursed God.

"Has anyone informed my son Basha about the accident?" questioned Shashi's mother, Parvathamma. No one spoke up.

"Have you informed your husband, Savitha?"

"No mother, I thought someone might have informed," answered Savitha politely.

"Ok, at least now you call him," cried Parvathamma.

Shashi was in a sorrowful mood.

"Why are you calling Basha, mother? He himself is in debt and needs money to get back his auto rickshaw from the mortgage. That's the reason he is driving auto rickshaw on a daily basis. How can he be helpful in arranging Rs. 5 lakhs," questioned Shashi.

"As an uncle, it is his right to know about Rohith's accident," cried Shashi's mother.

"Please call Basha Uncle, Ajith," requested Shashi's mother. Ajith took his mobile and called Basha.

Ajith calls Basha and hands over the phone to Parvathamma. Basha picked up the call.

"Hello Basha, where are you?" asked Parvathamma.

"I am in Koramangala police station," replied Basha.

"Do you know about the accident?" asked Parvathamma.

"Which accident?" asked Basha innocently.

"Shashi's son, Rohith met with an accident and he is in Modern Hospital, in a serious condition," explained Parvathamma.

"How? And when, Mother?" asked Basha.

"Doctors are asking Rs. 5 lakhs to do an operation on Rohith's head," cried Parvathamma.

"Ok Mother, I will be there in a minute," said Basha.

After a while, wearing a khaki uniform and holding a bundle in his hand Basha arrives. Savitha looks at Basha and whispers softly in Parvathamma's ear that her husband has arrived.

"Basha has arrived," cried Parvathamma.

Everyone looks at him causally, including Shashi and his wife. Basha comes near his mother and looks at Shashi, who was crying, holding his wife firmly.

"Where is Rohith? How is he?" Basha asked his mother.

"He is in the ICU. Doctors are asking to deposit Rs. 5 lakhs," cried Parvathamma.

Basha hands over the bundle to his mother and says "Take this money, this is Rs. 10 lakhs—Deposit Rs. 5 lakhs and keep the remaining Rs. 5 lakhs for the expenses."

Shashi and all the family members are extremely surprised and are wondering how Basha managed to arrange such a huge amount in such a less time.

Shashi gets up, leaving his wife on floor and starts to argue with Basha.

"From where did you get this much money? Did you rob or something?" asked Shashi.

"No, my brother, I haven't robbed," replied Basha politely.

"Then how? Or did you get involved in some illegal activities?" asked Shashi in very condemning manner.

"It's a big story, please trust me, brother," said Basha passing his hand through his hair in a tense manner.

"Shashi, now is not the time to discuss how he got the money," said Parvathamma.

"You first pay the amount in the hospital. Brother, as of now, I can't explain how I got the amount," said Basha.

"First, I have to go to the police station and after returning, I will tell in detail," said Basha.

In a few seconds, he departed from the hospital.

"He himself is having a huge credit on his auto rickshaw, so how did he get so much cash?" said one of the family members.

"Yes, that's true. How did he manage Rs. 10 lakhs?" murmured another family member.

"God only knows, we will come to know about this amount later, perhaps."

Let us see how Basha got the money.

Chapter 8

KISMAT (FATE)

It is yet early Monday morning and the rain that had started around 9 pm on Sunday night, has stopped. It is a typical Indian house, with two bedrooms and one drawing room and a kitchen. One bedroom is for Parvathamma and the other bedroom, for Basha and his wife. Basha, wearing a sleeveless vest comes out of the toilet and takes his mobile to call Shashi.

After two to three rings, Shashi picks up the phone.

"Hello brother," said Basha, the voice sounded muffled as it was in a loudspeaker mode.

"Uhh…Hello brother," answered Shashi in a low voice, after a few seconds.

"What's the reason for calling me?" questioned Shashi.

"Have you had your coffee and breakfast?" asked Basha is a pleasant tone.

"Yeah, I am having tea right now," said Shashi.

"Has Rohith got up?" asked Basha.

"Yeah, he is getting ready for school. Hmm…why did you call me?" asked Shashi in a frustrated voice.

"Nothing, I just need you to write a letter on behalf of me," requested Basha in a pleasant tone.

"Ok, are you in the house or in the police station?" asked Shashi.

"At the house and how did you guess, brother?" said Basha a bit puzzled.

"Somehow, and by the way, why are you opposing the corporation people?" asked Shashi in a frustrated voice.

"No my brother," said Basha politely. "I am not opposing the municipal people, I am only against the cutting of trees, which are harmless."

"Who are you to oppose? The tree is on the road and the corporation people have the right to cut down the tree. If it was in your land then the reason for your opposing would have been fair enough," said Shashi in an irritated voice.

"It's not the matter of the tree being on our land or on the government property," argued Basha. "You know that the tree was planted by our grandparents and we have spent our childhood days under the tree. The only reason for cutting down that tree is because it is blocking the view of the shopping mall and the corporation officials are in favor of the shopping mall."

***

"Ok you win, it's useless talking to people like you," said Shashi. "What's the matter to be written anyway?"

Basha said, "I just need you to write a letter against A.E. Basavaraju to the corporation commissioner. Even though there is a stay order on cutting down of the tree, he is ignoring the stay order and attempting to cut it down. A severe legal action must be taken against them by the commissioner."

"Why are you wasting your time and money for the trees?" suggested Shashi in an arguing voice.

"My brother! Trees are very useful for mankind. They provide us with many useful things without expecting anything from us. But we, instead of protecting them, we are cutting down the trees as if they are our enemies. Even then, they stand firm without complaining. We, being the dominant species of the planet, it is our duty to protect and preserve nature."

"Ok…ok you just protect, but I have no time to talk," replied Shashi.

There was a pause for a few seconds in the conversation.

Then Shashi said, "I will write the letter on behalf, but I won't be available in the house, so come and collect the letter from my wife. Ok bye."

"Thank you, my brother," said Basha, politely. Shashi cuts the call.

In a few minutes, Basha gets ready for his duty and walks out of the house. As he walks out of the house, he is surprised to see his daughter drawing Rangoli.

Rangoli is a folk art in India. Rangolis are decorated designs, made on the floor of living rooms, courtyards, in front of the doors and the gates, by Indian woman with rice powder or dhal (pulses).

This rice powder or dhal becomes the main food supplement for ants and small insects, and it is one of the best ways to feed some members of the animal kingdom around us.

The main reason for drawing Rangoli in front of main doors, is to welcome God or angels into our house to bring good fortunes into our house.

"Oh! What is this? Today my daughter is drawing Rangoli," said Basha, in excitement looking at his daughter.

"Yes, in her school there is a Rangoli competition. For that she is practicing Rangoli," said Savitha, who was busy in the kitchen. Basha's daughter, Aishwarya, looks at her father shyly and continues drawing Rangoli.

Aishwarya was a twelve years old child with sparkling eyes, long curly hair, straight nose, very fair complexion and wore a pair of hanging earrings, which made her look like a little angel.

"From today, I want my daughter to draw Rangoli for every occasion," said Basha, facing the kitchen's window and looking at Savitha. "It is good to see my child drawing Rangoli," he says with a smile on his face and he walks out of the house to start his auto rickshaw.

"At least have breakfast?" said Savitha, from the kitchen.

"It will become late for the commissioner's office," said Basha. "I have to collect the letter from Shashi's house too."

After starting the auto rickshaw, Basha looks at his daughter, Aishwarya.

And his daughter in turn looks at her father shyly and continues drawing Rangoli.

Basha captures the image of his daughter with the sparkling face, in his eyes and departs from his house.

After a while Basha collects the letter from Shashi's house and registers the complaint against Basavaraju to the BBMP commissioner's office.

After complaining, he returns to his regular auto rickshaw duty.

Chapter 9

A well middle-aged man, 50 years of age, named Narayan Mohan was standing at the bus stand waiting for an auto rickshaw. He was a tall man with a big head with white hair, piercing hazel eyes, trimmed white beard, big mouth, wearing a casual white shirt and pant and a woolen muffler around his neck. All in all, he was a well-built disciplined middle-aged man. He was going to MG Road to dump the dolls at wholesale price.

Narayan Mohan shouts and calls for the auto for a ride to MG Road. Many auto rickshaws reject Narayan Mohan's request for MG Road saying that there wouldn't be any return customers from MG Road during morning session. And a few others demanded double the meter-charge for MG Road. After a long while, Basha's empty auto comes across Narayan Mohan at the bus stand. Frustrated, Narayan Mohan was now willing to pay double the meter-charge, so he calls Basha's auto rickshaw. Basha stops his auto near Narayan Mohan.

"Will you go to MG Road?" asked Narayan Mohan.

"Yes, Sir," replied Basha very politely.

"I won't give double the fair," said Narayan Mohan.

"Just give the fare amount, Sir," said Basha.

Narayan Mohan is in a surprise as he loads the bundle of dolls into the auto and sits next to it in the passenger seat.

Basha tunes the meter to minimum fare and they depart from the bus stand.

While driving, Narayan Mohan starts talking to Basha.

"Hello Sir, usually auto drivers ask double the amount during morning session to MG Road," said Narayan Mohan curiously. "It is surprising that you didn't ask for double the fare."

"I abide by the principle of 'truth alone triumphs.' So, I never ask for double the fare from anyone," replied Basha.

"It is very rare to see people like you nowadays," said Narayan Mohan in a pleasing voice. During the travel, Basha's auto halts at a traffic signal. It is one of the busiest traffic signals in the city and usually the vehicles have to wait for three minutes to clear one side of the traffic. Since it was around 10 am in the morning, the traffic was at its peak. In India, it has become a tradition for the beggars to beg at traffic signals.

As usual, the beggars were begging at the traffic signal. One beggar named Vijay approached Basha's auto and started to beg for money. The beggar was a tall thin teenage boy, around 19 years of age, with medium shoulders, thick dusty hair spikes on his head. Pimples were forming on his nose and chin.

He was wearing a torn patched shirt and pant that was folded up to his knee. Altogether, he was looking like a poor hungry beggar.

"I haven't had food from last 3 days Sir, please give me money, Sir," said Vijay in a hungry voice.

Like this, Vijay begged from vehicle to vehicle until he reached Basha's auto rickshaw.

"Hey! Aren't ashamed to beg?" scolded Basha. "You look fit and fine. If you go for work you could easily earn your livelihood, then why are you begging?" He gave a glance to his passenger, expecting that even he might advise the beggar.

"Sir, at first I was ashamed of begging and so I tried to work. But no one gave me any work, those who gave work, used me for illegal activities or they didn't pay salary. If you're willing to offer money, then give me. Else, don't waste your time and mine, in advising," argued Vijay. "Advising is easy but to follow according to that, is difficult."

"If no one offered you any job, then why didn't you work on your own?" said Basha.

"Who would help me financially?" said Vijay.

"Will you help me? No, you won't. Giving advice is easy but helping is difficult," he said with a teasing smile. There was a pause for a few seconds in conversion.

Basha gives a glance to Narayan Mohan and bundle of dolls, who then speaks.

"If I give you these dolls to sell, will you be able to sell them?" asked Basha, pointing to the bundle of dolls in the back seat. Again, there was a silence for a few seconds. There was a smile on the face of Narayan Mohan, who was now looking at Vijay.

Gathering all his courage, Vijay said "Yes, I will sell these dolls."

"Basha facing Narayan Mohan Sir, will you please give 20 dolls at wholesale price?" requested Basha.

"With pleasure," said Narayan Mohan, patting encouragingly on the shoulder of Basha.

The traffic signal lights turn green and this was the omen of a good beginning. Basha requests Vijay to meet him in a corner of the road to collect the dolls.

Basha, Narayan Mohan and Vijay standing in a corner of the road.

"Sir, every piece of doll we usually sell at a wholesale price of Rs. 30, but for your sake, I will give them to you at Rs. 28," said Narayan Mohan.

"Will you please give 20 pieces of dolls?" requested Basha. "Yes Sir, for 20 pieces it will be Rs. 560, and you can sell each doll for Rs. 60 to Rs. 70, depending upon your marketing abilities."

"Ok...thanks for providing the concession," said Basha.

Turning towards Vijay, Basha says, "See, if you are willing to work hard sincerely, this is your chance."

Basha takes out the money from his pocket and gives Rs. 560 to Narayan Mohan and asks Narayan Mohan to give 20 pieces of dolls.

Basha said to Vijay, "See, even I don't have money. I am also in debt, so after selling these dolls, please return the Rs. 560 when I return in the evening and keep the profit for yourself."

"Sure, I will return your portion of money, Sir," said Vijay.

Taking the prettiest yellow doll in his hand, Basha says "One more thing, these dolls have very good messages written on their fur. So it will be better to sell these dolls requesting them to present these dolls to the ones they hate the most so that they start loving you."

"As you say, Sir," said Vijay. "Take the mobile number of Narayan Mohan for buying more toys in the future," said Basha. And after a while, Basha and the passenger Narayan Mohan left Vijay.

Narayan Mohan again starts speaking with Basha, "Hello Sir, what if he doesn't return your money and runs away with the money after selling the dolls?" said Narayan Mohan.

"If you would not have advised him and instead just offered him a rupee or two, you would have saved Rs. 560."

"I haven't helped him thinking that he should return the money. If I have to help others in future it is up to him. He must return the amount or I might lose faith in helping."

"It is also his final chance to improve his lifestyle. If he doesn't return, he will never be able to face me in his life and he won't get another chance to improve his life. And this truth will not allow him to sleep peacefully. I have done my share of good so far that God will give me double the money one day or the other."

"You are very good at heart" said Narayan Mohan. "And good things always happen to good people. But I am sure he will return your money," he pats the shoulder of Basha encouragingly. After accepting the challenge, Vijay sincerely started to work hard to sell the dolls at the busy traffic signal. After a while, selling two to three dolls, Vijay's confidence level increases and he starts marketing vigorously. His marketing technique was Basha's advice.

"Please present this doll to the one you hate the most so that they start loving you."

After a while, a Honda Activa rider named Pankaj halts at the same signal. He was a tall man in his forties, with small shoulders, with black and white hair, a firm moustache with wheatish skin tone, wearing a well ironed light-blue shirt and navy-blue pant. Vijay looks at Pankaj and approaches him and starts selling the doll. Initially, Pankaj ignores Vijay and his dolls. But when Vijay says, "Sir, if you buy this doll and present to the one who hates you the most and see the result." Hearing the word 'hate', Pankaj gets reminded of his office boss, who usually hated Pankaj in the office.

Pankaj gets impressed by the words of Vijay and shows interest in purchasing the doll.

"Sir please...please buy this doll," Vijay insists. "I am not begging for money, I am selling these dolls to make a living, so please help me. Sir, you won't find this type of doll at Rs. 60 in the market."

"What's the price of one piece?" asked Pankaj.

"One piece is Rs. 60, Sir," replied Vijay.

"What's the price for 2 pieces?" asked Pankaj.

"If you buy two pieces, I will give it to you for Rs. 110."

"Ok, tell me the final price of one piece, and I won't bargain."

"It is Rs. 60," said Vijay.

"I will give only Rs. 50," said Pankaj.

"Sir, in the market, the same doll is around Rs. 80 to Rs. 100."

"No, I have only Rs. 50," said Pankaj.

"Ok... give Rs. 5 extra, Sir," requested Vijay.

Vijay asks Pankaj to select the doll from the dolls.

Pankaj points to a yellow color doll. Vijay picks the doll and gives it to Pankaj. It was the same doll that was picked by Basha while advising Vijay about the marketing tactics. "Sir, please present this doll to the one who hates you the most and see they won't hate you further," said Vijay.

"Ok...let's see," said Pankaj.

Pankaj pays Rs. 50 to Vijay for the doll.

Vijay requests him for Rs. 5 more, but Pankaj refuses saying that he did not have any change.

"Ok…have a nice day," wished Vijay happily. The traffic signal turns green and Pankaj speeds away, taking the doll. Vijay continues to market and sell the dolls.

Chapter 10

Pankaj, who had just bought the yellow doll with the message 'My child is always a child to me' reaches his company's two-wheeler parking lot. After parking his vehicle, he takes a couple of files and the doll, and rushes to the office. As Pankaj was in a hurry, he doesn't notice the presence of his friend, Manoj.

"Hey Pankaj what's the hurry?" asked Manoj. "You didn't even bother to see me, what's the deal?"

"Hi Manoj, sorry but I am in a bit of hurry," apologized Pankaj.

"You are well on time, then why are you hurrying?" asked Manoj.

"I have to submit this file before my boss arrives," said Pankaj.

"Is it such a difficult task to submit this file?" asked Manoj.

"You don't know my boss, dude," said Pankaj.

"Sorry, I didn't get you," said Manoj.

"My boss is a very high-tempered man," explained Pankaj. "He always scolds and harasses his subordinates. Particularly in my case, he hates my work, degrades me and always tries to find a mistake in my work."

"Really? What you are saying?" asked Manoj.

"Yes, it's true, and it is getting late. Before my boss arrives; I have to submit this file on his desk," said Pankaj and departs for the office.

As soon as Pankaj enters the office, he directly walks into the boss' chamber to submit the file on his desk. After placing the files on the desk, he walks out of the chamber in a hurry, forgetfully placing the doll on the desk. After a while, the manager arrives in the office, carrying an official suitcase in his hand and a tensed look on his face. All employees of the office stand up in respect. The manager's name is Karan Saxena. He was a tall man with broad shoulders and a moderately well-built body. He had brownish eyes, thick black hair, a very fair complexion, a sharp pointing nose, with no moustache and yet he was a good-looking man in his fifties.

Karan gets into his chamber. Some people in the office signal to their colleagues that the boss is in a very angry mood and one of them is going to get a sound scolding from him.

As soon as Karan enters his chamber, he rings the call-bell. The peon rushes inside the chamber and comes out in two seconds.

"Sir, the boss is calling you," said the peon to Pankaj.

Pankaj thinks to himself that when all the files have been correctly and timely submitted, what could possibly be the reason for calling him inside so early.

Pankaj reaches the chamber of Karan Saxena.

"May I come in, Sir?" asked Pankaj. There was no response. So Pankaj gathers all his courage and enters. As soon as he enters the chamber, he realizes his mistake when he sees the doll on Karan's desk, which he had placed there by mistake, while arranging the files earlier.

"Did you come to my chamber earlier?" asked Karan in a commanding voice, as he was going through the files.

"Yes, Sir," said Pankaj in a whisper. "Did you keep this doll on my table?" asked Karan.

Pankaj stammered in fear and said, "Y....yes Sir."

He shouts in anger and bangs the file on the desk and says "What do you think of my chamber? This is an office and not a kinder-garden, you fool. You don't have any sense and what's the meaning of this doll, you idiot?"

Pankaj is fear-struck, confused and unable to say anything. Understanding the intensity of his boss' anger, he starts to lie so as to cover up for his mistake.

"Sir, today was my son's birthday," cried Pankaj. "So, he presented me this doll and asked me to give it in the office to the one person whom I respected the most. So, I thought it good to give it to you."

"Is this true or are you just making up a nice story?" asked Karan.

"No, Sir," said Pankaj.

"Being well educated, you don't have even this much common sense?" said Karan. "On the birthday of a person, we must give a gift to the birthday boy and not the other way round."

"If it really is your son's birthday today, go and present him a gift in the evening."

"Yes, Sir," replied Pankaj.

"Keep the suitcase below," commanded Karan. Karan picks up the files and goes through them. Pankaj takes the suitcase and the doll and keeps them below the desk and stands still.

"Ok, you can go now," said Karan, "But do not try to act smart with me once again."

Pankaj walks out of Karan's chamber. While Karan goes through the files, the words of Pankaj echo in his mind.

"My son's birthday."

"My son's birthday."

Karan's mind was unable to concentrate on the files, so he leans back onto his chair, while his mind is unable to settle down. It keeps wandering over and over, thinking about the morning incident at his house between him and his son. He slowly closes his eyes and places his interlocked fingers at the back of his head.

It is Monday morning around 7:30 am.

Karan Saxena enters his house in the jogging dress. The house is a well-built duplex, with a big car parking space and a small garden surrounded by a brick compound. Inside the house, there is a kitchen, big living room, dining hall, Karan's bedroom and a staircase which leads into the first floor. On the first floor, there are two large bedrooms; one is for guests and the other is for Karan's son, Adithya. As soon as Karan enters the house, his worker, Ranganna brought him a hand towel and a newspaper. Ranganna was a short old man in his sixties with a moderate personality; he was still active in the household works, with hard fists and forearms. Karan receives the hand towel and newspaper and sits on the chair.

"Has Adithya woken up?" asked Karan.

"Yes, my lord," replied Ranganna.

"Where is he?" asked Karan.

"He is in his room," replied Ranganna.

"Adithya, come here," shouted Karan in a high-pitch voice. Ranganna, who was standing there, returned to the kitchen realizing that Karan was angry. Adithya comes down from the upstairs very slowly, as if in fear. He was a tall young boy, with board shoulders, thick black hair, fair complexion, a pointed nose, flat stomach, trimmed moustache and beard, wearing a round neck T-shirt, shorts and a sports-watch. Simply put, he was a normal college-going boy.

"Where were you yesterday after college?" asked Karan in commanding voice.

Adithya initially hesitates to speak. He finally says, "After college, there was no special class, so…"

"What so…so…? You went for a movie and you didn't even bother to inform me," scolded Karan. He continued, "Your professor met me in the morning at the park and where did you get money for the tickets?" There was a pause for two seconds.

"Speak out," shouted Karan in a high-pitch voice.

"My classmates shared the ticket price," cried Adithya.

"Oh, your friends shared your ticket price? Now you missed one special class and went for a movie, do you know the loss of that class?"

"Father, it was only one movie," cried Adithya.

"Every bad habit starts small and later it grows big," shouted Karan.

"Father, I am 22 years old boy. Do you yet think I am a child?" cried Adithya. "Even the selection of my course is made by you. You didn't even bother to ask me which course I was interested in," argued Aditya. "When I was at your age, no one guided me," said Karan. "If anyone like myself would have guided me, perhaps I would have been an IAS officer. So, I didn't want you to suffer like me."

"Father, I am not interested in that course," cried Adithya. "If I don't have freedom for selection of my course or to even watch my favorite movie, then it is a waste of life."

"Yes, it is better for such children, like you, to die than give pain to their parents," shouted Karan, throwing the paper on Adithya's face and walking into his room.

Karan wakes up from the dream state. The clock bell rings 5 o' clock and Karan picks up the suitcase and departs from the office to his house. It was around 6:30 in the evening.

Adithya was looking for his father's car from his window as if he was waiting for him to arrive. After a while, Karan's car entered the gate. Karan parks the car, enters the house, sits on the sofa and removes his shoes.

Ranganna approaches him and stands with folded hands.

"Get me coffee," ordered Karan to Ranganna. "My lord, Adithya hasn't had food since morning," said Ranganna in a low voice.

"So what should I do? Feed him with my hands?" said Karan in a rude voice.

"Go bring me coffee," ordered Karan.

Ranganna goes inside the kitchen. After removing his shoes, Karan opens the suitcase, and to his surprise he finds the yellow doll with the message "My child is always a child to me." Karan murmured to himself "You idiot, Pankaj, you must have kept the doll inside this suitcase."

Karan took out the doll from the suitcase and started reading the message "My child is always a child to me." After reading it, he realizes that he had scolded his son for nothing, in the morning. He realizes that there is one nice way to console his son—by presenting him the doll. So, he keeps the doll inside the suitcase and takes out the files and calls Adithya.

"Adi...Adithya, come here," shouted Karan.

Ranganna serves the coffee to Karan. Adithya walks down from the stairs slowly, wearing shorts and T-shirt and stands in front of his father hanging his head low.

"Adi, I have brought something for you. It is inside my suitcase, take it," said Karan. Adithya looks at his father for a while, who is busy concentrating on the files and having coffee. Adithya bends down and opens the suitcase, and to his surprise, he sees the yellow doll in the suitcase. Adithya reads the message on the doll—'My child is always a child to me.' After reading it, he looks at his father for a while. He then cries out loudly and falls to the legs of his father, holding his father's feet firmly.

"Adi, what happened? Why are you crying? What is the reason, please tell me," asked Karan in a surprise. "Forgive me, father, forgive me, please forgive me, I won't do it again," cried Adithya.

"What are you saying?" said Karan. "It was me who was rude to you in the morning. I was not able to understand your feelings in the morning. So, I am the one who should feel sorry."

"No dad, no. It is you, who has to forgive me for the deed which I was going to commit, which might have taken your life."

"Adi, what are you talking about?" asked Karan shockingly. "I don't understand, Adi. Please calm down and tell me exactly what happened."

Then Adithya hugs his father very firmly and says, "Please forgive me father, please..."

"Control yourself, Adi. Don't be so emotional. Am I not saying that it was my mistake in the morning?"

"No dad, it was me," said Adithya, holding his father's hand he takes him to his bedroom. Seeing this, even Ranganna's eyes get moist and he follows them.

"Why you are so emotional, Adi?" asked Karan.

Adithya opens his room door and takes his father inside. As soon as Karan enters the room, he gets a shock, looking at the hanging rope from the ceiling fan. Tears start to flow from his eyes and he started to cry, hugging his son very firmly.

"Why Adi, why?" cried Karan. Since morning I was not able to console myself and I was very upset about this morning. So I decided to kill myself (suicide). I even wrote a suicide note saying that no one was responsible for my death. I was just waiting for your arrival, to see your face for the last time. But I didn't know that you still loved me like a small child and brought me that doll." Both sat on the bed. Ranganna enters inside the bedroom, removes the hanging rope from the ceiling fan and takes the suicide note outside the house and burned both the letter and the rope. Then the worker returns to the bedroom.

Adithya is sleeping on the lap of Karan.

"Ranganna, do we have any sweet dish for dinner?" asked Karan in an excited voice.

"I am overwhelmed by seeing the father and son affection, and so I need rest today. Let's go to the temple and have dinner in a restaurant," said Ranganna in excitement. Karan chuckles in happiness. After a while, Ranganna takes Adithya for bath, who was still crying on the lap of his father. Karan, seeing the doll for a while hears an inner voice.

"Thank you, my friend Pankaj. Till now, I was scolding you for nothing, but today knowingly or unknowingly you have saved my son's life, and for that I am and will be ever grateful to you throughout my life."

After a while they visited to the nearby temple and later had dinner at a restaurant.

Chapter 11

It is around 10 pm on Monday night and there is a dark room with a single hanging bulb. Below the burning bulb is a wooden table surrounded by five people, standing around the table. The bulb is the only source of light in the room. One of the men was tall, with broad shoulders, strong arms, and large head with a huge stomach. The 2nd man was a tall man, with narrow shoulders, a lean personality, a flat chest and a flat stomach and an unshaved beard of two weeks. The 3rd man was a short man with proportional shoulders to his height. He looked like an average fit man with a trimmed beard and a thick moustache. All the three of them were in their thirties.

The 4th man was a teenager, about 18-19 years of age with thick black hair, firm mouth, uncleaned teeth with tobacco residue, slim body with average height. The most interesting man was the fifth man as he was a tall man, with a straight nose, sharp piercing eyes, firm mouth, very calm, a man known to take charge. And he was the leader of their gang. The leader said, "This is the road she usually takes to college" said the leader (pointing to the sketch on the table). This is the place where we attack her. If we miss her, we must complete the job on the spot itself.

Man 1: Ok, boss.

Pointing to the Man 3, "Hey, you must drive the car and shouldn't get down from the car. Remember… the car must be quick in the traffic." Leader pointing to Man 1 and Man 2 says, "You both must be very quick to grab her," suggested their leader. "After catching, you must hold tightly till I get down from car." Pointing to Man 4, he says, "You must assist me, after the task is completed. We must head on this road towards Andhra border."

"Is it necessary to go so far?" asked Man 2. "If suppose police come to know, we must be well prepared," said leader. Anyway, it is a well prepared plan, nothing can go wrong. Success is guaranteed."

"Do you have the victim's photo, boss?" asked Man 2. Leader takes out the photo from his upper shirt pocket and throws on the table. Everyone's eyes stare at the photo.

It was around 9:30 am, on Tuesday morning. The atmosphere was different from the previous day as it was a bright sunny morning, and yet the college bell hadn't rung. Three students carrying college-bags entered the college toilet in a suspicious manner. One of the students was Siddharth. He was a tall young guy of 20 years with a flat stomach and chest, very lean arms, spiked hair, piercing in one of his ears, big mouth, no moustache and a short beard, wearing a T-shirt and jeans, holding his bag carefully. Another student was Mukesh. He was a tall handsome boy with trimmed moustache and beard, small build, thick black hair, straight nose, wearing a colored T-shirt and jeans. The third student was Prashanth. He was a short boy, good looking with a narrow moustache, flat stomach, small straight nose, wearing a colored T-shirt and jeans. After the three students entered the toilet, Siddharth realizes that the all the toilet cabins are empty and he points to one of the corner toilet cabin.

"This cabin is best suited," said Siddharth in a fearing voice.

"Have you brought it, my friend?" asked Mukesh.

"Yes, it was very difficult, but somehow I managed to get it," replied Siddharth in a whisper.

"Please take it out," requested Mukesh.

"Sure….! It's highly concentrated," explained Siddharth. "Remove it very cautiously because even one drop of it can burn a hole into the body, so handle it very carefully."

Siddharth takes out a bottle of highly concentrated sulphuric acid from his college bag. Mukesh, then slowly takes it from Siddharth.

"Mukesh, I think what you are going to do is wrong, my friend," suggested Prashanth.

"Even I think the same," supported Siddharth.

"If you think that what I am going to do is wrong, then what you think she is doing? Is that fair?" asked Mukesh.

"You both know that how much I love her…" He pulls out his T-shirt showing the tattoo of her face. "From the moment I saw her, I am in love with her. I think even she was in love with me. After roaming with me for a while, when I proposed to her, she rejected me saying that she had never loved me and that her career was more important."

"Even I think that she was not in love with you, my friend," advised Prashanth.

Mukesh said, "You won't understand my pain, you don't know what I am going through. It is such that it cannot be explained. I can't eat, sleep, think or even concentrate on my studies. She thinks that she is the queen of the college and so she is very proud of her beauty. I will make her beauty disappear; she will have to suffer throughout her life for not loving me."

"What you are saying is wrong," said Prashanth. "It might be true that she was your friend and you unknowingly might have loved her. Yours was a one-sided love. Love doesn't exist by force. Love is the union of two hearts."

"Prashanth, you are not understanding my pain, what you are saying might be true but I cannot live without her," cried Mukesh.

"Just be patient for a few days, then you will realize the grave mistake (sin) you were about to commit," said Prashanth.

"Please Prashanth, you cannot change my decision by advising," cried Mukesh. "Whatever be it, but I am throwing acid on her face. If you are my true friends, you will support me, right?"

"I am your true friend, that's why I am advising you," argued Prashanth.

"The sin which you are going to commit is going to ruin both your lives. It would be better to kill her instead of throwing acid on her face. I am not going to support your foolish decision, I am sorry."

"Will you support me?" asked Mukesh to Siddharth.

"Yes, my friend," replied Siddharth.

Prashanth walked out of the toilet. Mukesh and Siddharth also went out of the toilet as it was time for Roopa's arrival.

Adithya, who was in one of the toilet cabins all this while, slowly comes out with a fear, looking if Mukesh and Siddharth are still in the toilet. Adithya, who had heard all the conversations of Mukesh, Siddharth and Prashanth, plans to save Roopa Kulkarni. Roopa, with her two friends is having a conversation of their own, roaming in the college campus where most of the students weren't present. Roopa was a very young beautiful girl, with long untied black hair, small beautiful nose, very fair complexion, pearl-like piercing eyes, well darkened eyebrows, rose-petal lips, snail-shell neck and a beautiful face. She was the college queen and every boy in the college was a fan of her beauty.

Mukesh and Siddharth come from behind Roopa.

"Roopa...Roopa," shouted Mukesh.

Roopa turns back to face Mukesh.

"I wanted to talk with you alone," demanded Mukesh.

"What's the reason?" asked Roopa.

"It's personal," replied Mukesh.

"See Mukesh, I was not in love with you," said Roopa politely. "So, please don't disturb me again. I have to concentrate on my studies. If you disturb me again, I am going to complaint to the principal."

"You don't love..." shouted Mukesh, like a psychopath.

Mukesh took out the acid bottle from his pocket and opened the lid of the bottle. Roopa and her friends, sensing the danger, scream for help. As Mukesh throws the acid on Roopa's face, Adithya interferes in between them at a terrifying speed, pushing Roopa down. The acid fell on the shoulder of Adithya. It was a narrow escape for Roopa. Roopa's friends ran, screaming for help. Adithya, who was in pain asked Roopa to run away. Mukesh was in a shock and looked at Adithya in surprise. Roopa rushed from the spot in fear towards the college main gate. Even Mukesh followed her and chased her, holding the remaining acid in the bottle in his hand.

As Roopa was running, her feet stumbled upon a stone and she fell down. Mukesh reached her very quickly and teased her with his evil intentions.

"Please don't do this, Mukesh" pleaded Roopa, folding both her palms together. And, there was no one to help Roopa.

Mukesh, without any mercy, positioned the acid bottle and was about to throw it on Roopa's face. Suddenly, an Omni van comes from behind Mukesh, hitting him on his back. Acid falls on his chest and shoulder. Mukesh is in pain and starts to shout and yell.

Two to three men wearing monkey-caps get down from the black Omni van and abducted Roopa. Within a fraction of a second, Roopa is saved from the acid attack and she is abducted by the kidnappers. The Omni van vanishes into the city traffic very quickly.

Chapter 12

It was around 11:00 pm in Roopa Kulkarni's house. Roopa Kulkarni's house was a big luxurious house, a three-floored bungalow, having a garden in front of the house, a swimming pool and two Mercedes cars parked in the parking slot. Anyone can estimate their standard and their huge income just by looking at the palatial bungalow. The family members of Roopa Kulkarni were grieving. Among the family members, her father, Rajath Kulkarni and her mother, Mamtha Kulkarni were crying and were very upset about the unfortunate incidents. Even the police were already present in Roopa's house with their usual tracking equipment and were interviewing every member of the family, as per the law.

Rajath Kulkarni was a big tall man with broad shoulders, fair complexion and wearing a creamy kurta. He was a rich man with a big charming personality. Mamtha Kulkarni was a big plump woman, with fair complexion and a beautiful face. She was a rich chubby married woman.

Other than Roopa's parents, a couple of her cousins were also present in the house. "Do not worry, nothing will happen to your daughter," said inspector Arjun Kumar. Inspector was a tall man with clean shaved face and a well-built physique.

"How can we not worry?" said Rajath Kulkarni. "She is our only daughter, firstly she escaped from the acid attack and later she was kidnapped and still you don't know who the kidnappers are. Nor do you know their motive."

"Sir, please co-operate with us" replied inspector Arjun. "If you yourself get angry, then how can we help? "We are investigating the students who tried to attack Roopa with the acid, and even the boy, who saved your daughter. But unfortunately the kidnappers are very intelligent as they have changed the car's number plate. That's the reason we are unable to track them down."

"Sir, please be honest, do you have any enemies in business or in your personal life, because if the kidnappers would have abducted your daughter for a ransom, then they should have called you by now."

Then suddenly the mobile of Rajath Kulkarni rang. Rajath Kulkarni looks at the screen of the mobile and screams "It's my daughter, Roopa."

"Who's call?" questioned the inspector.

"It's from my daughter," screamed Rajath Kulkarni. Roopa's mother rushed to grab the mobile.

"Wait a minute, put it on loudspeaker," said the inspector. Rajath Kulkarni puts the call on loudspeaker.

"Hello, hello…Roopa…Roopa, my daughter! Are you safe? Speak up…Hello…hello," cried Rajath Kulkarni. On the other end of the call, there was total silence. Rajath looks towards the inspector.

"No one is speaking," Inspector signals to wait. After a few seconds, a male voice spoke "Hello, is this Rajath Kulkarni?" asked the gang leader.

"Yes, who are you?" asked Rajath in a sobbing voice.

"I am one of the kidnappers who kidnapped your daughter," replied the gang leader.

"Why have you kidnapped my daughter?" cried Rajath. "Is it for money? I will give you anything, but please don't do anything to my daughter."

"It is in your hands if you want your daughter to return safely to your house," said leader.

"I will do as you say, please don't harm her," pleaded Rajath.

"We just need Rs. 50 lakhs in cash and please do not go to the police and try to seek help from them. If the police are already informed, request them not to involve themselves any further. Make arrangements for the money and note that I want the cash only in the denomination of 1,000s, without staple pins. I will call you after some time."

"Hello, hello Sir, my wife wants to talk to Roopa, please Sir," requested Rajath.

"Don't worry, she is perfectly alright. She will return to your home safely without a scratch, in the evening, if you deliver the money as per my conditions. Okay, be ready with the cash," said the leader.

"Ok please…please," cried Rajath and the call ends.

Rajath and his wife cried out, worrying about their daughter. Inspector asked a policeman if he had traced the call.

"Yes Sir, the signal is from Malur area i.e., near Andhra Pradesh border."

"Can you try and find out where the mobile is currently, or in which signal range does it fall?"

"The number has been switched off, Sir."

"Alert the Malur area police (near A.P.) and ask them to search the whole area and nab the suspects with a black Omni van," ordered the inspector.

The cousins of Rajath look at the inspector with fear and take Rajath to a side.

"Let us give the money to the kidnappers and bring back our daughter safely," advised cousin (1) to Rajath Kulkarni.

"Do you remember what the kidnappers told? Let's request the police not to interfere further until our daughter reaches us safely," said cousin (2).

"Yes," agreed cousin (1).

Rajath holding his forehead and thinking, slowly walked towards the police men.

"Sir, we have decided to give Rs. 50 lakhs to the kidnappers and we are asking your help of not getting involved further in this case, as it might affect our daughter's well-being," requested Rajath.

"What are you saying, Sir? We are trying to help you and now you are saying not to get involved in this case?" said the S.I. (sub-inspector of police). S.I. Harish was a short man with a lean personality, an athletic body and he was in his uniform.

"It's okay, calm down," consoled the inspector to S.I. and then to Rajath.

"We understand your feelings. Let's wait until they call again, it is our duty to safeguard your daughter. Let's allow us to do our duty please, Sir," appealed the inspector.

"Whatever it is, Sir, please don't interfere in our matter now," said Rajath.

Rajath takes his wife to the bedroom. Inspector asks the S.I. to alert the police near the signal as soon as the call comes from the A.P. border. "Yes, Sir," said S.I. Harish.

Rajath Kulkarni, his wife, cousin and police were waiting for the call from the kidnappers, with Rs. 50 lakhs cash, ready in the bag. The mobile was on the table, all the members in the house were looking at each other and staring at the mobile to ring.

The mobile finally rings. Rajath picks the mobile in a hurry and activates the call.

"Hello, hello Sir, where to come?" cried Rajath.

"Hello Sir, be calm," said the gang leader. "First, ask the police not to involve any further in this case. Secondly, the money/money bag shouldn't have any transmitter. Thirdly, only you must come alone to hand over the money to us. If the police follow you, you won't be able to see your daughter face again. So understand we are not professional kidnappers, the circumstances have made us so. So, please understand the situation and behave properly."

"I will do as you say, please don't do anything to my daughter," requested Rajath.

"Ok," said the gang leader. "First, take the money in a bag and go to Mayo hall bus stand. Then I will call you 15 minutes later. Keep Rs. 100 note as a change in your pocket." The call ends.

Rajath says to the inspector, "Sir, will you please take out the transmitter from the money bag and leave us alone or I am going to call the commissioner to do so," said Rajath. "Not necessary, Sir," obeyed the inspector.

"What are you saying, Sir?" argued the S.I. "Yes, just follow my order leave now catch later," said the inspector. S.I. removes the transmitter from the money bag and then, the police men pack everything and gets out of the house.

Rajath takes the money bag and leaves out of the house and catches an auto rickshaw. S.I. Harish and inspector Arjun Kumar are in their police caravan. "How did they know about our transmitter?" asked the S.I. "I guess the kidnappers are from within the house" said the inspector and they know every details of our activities. Let us follow the Rajath and alert the police in the city at the A.P. border (Malur)."

In a few minutes, Rajath was at Mayo hall bus stand. As soon as he gets down from the auto, he gets a call from the gang leader.

"Are you there at the bus stand?" asked the gang leader.

"Yes, I am at the bus stop," replied Rajath.

"Ok, catch the next bus to Malur," commanded the gang leader.

"Ok…" said Rajath. And the call ends. Rajath waits for a while when finally bus to Malur comes and he catches the bus

The police caravan follows the bus and at the next stop inspector sends a mufti police man inside the bus to look after Rajath's activities. "Are you tracking the signal range?" asked inspector Arjun.

"Yes Sir, the signal is varying. In the morning, it was in Malur and now it is in between places like Mulabagilu and Bangarpet. I think they are moving and also their voice is different," explained a police man. "Ok… That's enough," said the inspector. Alert and keep track of every movement of the kidnappers and let's follow Rajath.

Rajath is sitting in the bus in a very tensed manner staring at his mobile screen very frequently. The mufti police in the bus stands, informs about every activity of Rajath to inspector Arjun through message. After a few minutes, his mobile rang in his hand and he picks up the call and talks.

"Hello Sir," said Rajath.

"Get down from the bus," said the gang leader. "Sir, still the Malur bus stand hasn't come," said Rajath. "It's Ok. Are you sure that the police is not following you?" asked in a high-pitch voice.

"I swear, I am sure police is not following me," replied Rajath, very kindly. "Give Rs. 100 to the bus conductor and ask him to stop the bus and get down immediately." Rajath gives Rs. 100 note to the bus conductor and asks him to stop the bus. The conductor blows the whistle and the bus stops. Rajath gets down from the bus.

"Ok, wait for another bus to come," said the gang leader. In the same manner, the kidnapper asked him to change 4-5 buses. Rajath, after changing the buses according to the instructions of the kidnapper, waits for Malur bus. After a while, he gets a call. "Hello Sir," said Rajath.

"Go back to Bangalore," said the gang leader.

"What happened, Sir? I think Malur is just ten kilometers from here," asked Rajath.

"I think the police is following you and us near the Malur border. The police activity is more intensive, so you just go back to Bangalore," said the gang leader.

"Sir, I don't know anything, please don't do anything to my daughter," requested Rajath.

"Just do as I say," shouted the gang leader.

"Ok, Sir," said Rajath emotionally. And the call ended.

As Rajath crosses the opposite side of the road, he gets the bus to Bangalore. The police man who was following Rajath in the bus returned to the police caravan and Inspector Arjun asks him about the details of Rajath's activities from the policeman who followed Rajath.

"I think the kidnappers have come to know that we are following them," said S.I. Harish.

"I don't think," said inspector. Actually, I think some someone close to Rajath is behind all this.

"Yes Sir, they must be very brilliant," said S.I.

"Then we must be more brilliant," replied the inspector.

Then suddenly on their police laptop screen, it shows that the gang leader is calling Rajath again.

"Sir, the kidnapper is calling again," said the police.

Gang leader says to Rajath, "Hello Rajath, you go to Indiranagar bus stand, my men will come on bike and take the money. And don't try to stop or talk to them. Only then will your daughter reach your home safely," ordered the gang leader.

"Ok, as you say, Sir," cried Rajath.

"Let's follow the bus," said the inspector.

"I think the kidnappers are actually foolish to come to Bangalore and fall in our trap," said S.I.

"I don't think so, let's follow the bus," said inspector.

After a few minutes, the bus reaches Indiranagar bus stand.

Rajath gets out of the bus and stands waiting at the bus stand for the kidnappers to arrive.

The police caravan which was following Rajath, waits for kidnappers and warns all the police in the city to be alert.

After a while, Rajath places the money bag between his legs. This was noticed by inspector Arjun from the caravan and he gets suspicious about the money bag being empty. Until then, Rajath was struggling to carry the fully loaded money bag, now he notices a change. So, the inspector gets out of the van and rushed towards Rajath. The S.I. tries to stop him, but in vain. Inspector reaches Rajath and opens the money bag and the money bag was empty. Inspector looks at Rajath in anger and frustration. Rajath gets a call from his wife that her daughter is back home safely.

"Ok, thank you Sir, my daughter is back home safely," said Rajath in a cheerful voice.

Rajath called out an auto rickshaw and departed from the bus stand. Irritated inspector asked the police to search the bus and the passengers.

He thinks that the kidnappers were in the returning bus and so asks the city police to search the persons who are suspicious.

"From where did the kidnappers come and how did they take the money?" asked S.I. Harish to himself, and inspector utterly confused of the incidents.

The inspector started to imagine how the kidnappers would have walked away with money. Rajath returns to the bus stand, later he catches the bus to Indiranagar, in which he sits in the last row of the bus. The passengers in the bus were very busy in their own activities. There were three young guys who were seated in the second last row, right in front of Rajath. Seeing this opportunity, the 1st youth gets up and goes to the last seat and shows Rajath his daughter's photo. The 2nd youth standing on the way and the other guy transfers the money from the money bag to the two sports bags. Then the 1st youth gets down taking one bag at K.R. Puram bus stand.

"Now, you will get a call, just say ok…ok?" said the 3rd youth.

"Ok, Sir," said Rajath.

Then Rajath gets the call from the gang leader, who then asks him to stand at Indiranagar bus stand. Rajath gets down from the bus at Indiranagar and the two young guys with the money bag get down at the next stop and catch an auto rickshaw. The two kidnappers keep the money bag at the back of the auto rickshaw's passenger seat. The bottom of the bag gets stuck to a bolt in the auto rickshaw and rips the bag.

As the auto rickshaw is going in the road, one kidnapper looks ahead at the police activities that are going on for every vehicle on the road. He signs to the other kidnapper and both panic.

"Hey, please drive fast to the railway station," requested one of the kidnappers very softly.

"Ok, Sir," said Basha.

Suddenly a tree branch falls down in front of the auto rickshaw with a sound similar to an explosion, blocking the entire road and bringing the traffic to a halt. Basha was in a shock and he rushed out of the auto to see what had happened. He stands there seeing the tree and the branch emotionally, with tears in his eyes. Slowly, the policemen and other people gather. The tree is the same tree which he had saved on Monday morning, but the branch is different. The branch which the corporation people had chopped to three-fourths was still firm on the tree. S.I. Ratnakar asks the constable to take the auto to the side of the road. Police constables ask the kidnappers, "Where is the auto driver?"

"He is in the crowed," replied one of the kidnappers. Police constable walks into the crowed. At this moment, kidnappers try to take the bag in a hurry and the bag rips further. They leave it there, fearing that police might catch them anytime now. Basha was feeling sad as he touched the branch of tree for a while.

"Wow...! You see, the tree might have fallen on your rickshaw if you were one second early. Your timing was good and so you escaped by a whisker," said constable 1.

"Ok, take the auto and help to clear the road block and traffic," said constable 2. Basha went to his auto rickshaw and said to the two kidnappers.

"Sir, please take another auto," requested Basha. I can't come, I have some important work to do," said Basha.

"Why didn't the three-fourth cut branch break? Why did the branch fall down right in front of me? What's the reason?" Basha emotionally asked himself.

Meanwhile, at the same time, on the walkie-talkie of the police constable, S.I Harish announced a message – "If any one sees anyone suspicious with bags, please arrest and investigate them."

The two kidnappers hearing the walkie-talkie message leave the bag at back of auto rickshaw.

"How much is the fare?" asked one of the kidnappers. "It's Ok, Sir," said Basha and refuses to take the money.

The two kidnappers started looking suspiciously at the back of the auto and departed from the spot. Later, the two kidnappers call their leader and narrate everything.

"You just wait and watch what happens and follow the auto, if anything goes wrong, just get out of there. We already have Rs. 25 lakhs," suggested the gang leader to the kidnappers.

"Ok, boss," said the kidnappers.

S.I. Ratnakar gets a call from his wife and he sits in the auto and continues to talk. Basha and the police constables, with the help of a few other people lift the tree branch and keep it on the side of the road. Basha returns to his auto rickshaw.

S.I Ratnakar says to Basha, "Hey you, drop me at the next market, my wife is waiting there."

S.I. Ratnakar says to police constable, "I will be back in a minute."

Basha starts the auto and in the mirror he sees the two kidnappers standing and staring the auto rickshaw from the corner of the road. When he turns back and sees them, the 2 kidnappers hide looking at Basha. The two kidnappers follow Basha's auto rickshaw. While traveling, S.I. Ratnakar touches the bag with his hand as he was talking on the mobile. Basha drops S.I. Ratnakar in the market and while returning, a passenger stops the auto.

"Will you go to city railway station?" asked the passenger.

"Yes," replied Basha. Then the passenger tries to keep the luggage at the back of auto rickshaw.

"Hey you, where do I keep the luggage," asked the passenger.

"Keep it at the back," said Basha looking in the front mirror.

"There is already a big bag," said the passenger. Basha walks out of auto to see the big bag. Looking at the money bag, Basha realizes that the two kidnappers had left the bag. Basha pulls out the bag with force and the bag tears, and a few Rs. 1000 bundles fall down. Then Basha drops the bag in shock.

After few seconds he speaks to himself.

"I think this money is not obtained by good deeds. So, the two guys must have left the bag," whispered Basha to himself.

"So, that is why they were staring at the auto and looking suspicious all the time. Fearing the police they abandoned the bag at the back of the rickshaw," said Basha to himself.

Now it is better to hand it over to the police or there might be more problems due to this money. Basha says to the passenger, "Please take another auto, Sir," requested Basha politely.

Then Basha started the auto and headed towards the police station and stops the auto in front of the police station and took the torn bag with bundles of currency notes inside it and started to walk towards the entrance of police station.

The two kidnappers who were following Basha realize that he was going to handover the money to the police, so they get out of there. As Basha steps inside the entrance of the police station, he gets a call from Ajith Kumar, which he picks. Then Basha takes a U-turn and heads towards the Modern Hospital.

Basha parks the auto in the parking lot of the Modern Hospital, and rushes towards the reception hall, holding a bundle of cash in his hand. Savitha, looking at Basha whispers silently in Parvathamma's ear.

"Basha has arrived," cried Parvathamma.

Everyone looks at him casually, including Shashi and his wife. Basha comes near his mother and looking at Shashi, who was crying, holding his wife firmly.

"Where is Rohith? How is he?" Basha asked his mother.

"He is in the ICU. Doctors are asking to deposit Rs. 5 lakh," cried Parvathamma.

Basha hands over the bundle to his mother and says, "Take this money, this is Rs. 10 lakhs—Deposit Rs. 5 lakhs and keep the remaining Rs. 5 lakhs for the expenses."

Shashi and all the family members are extremely surprised and are wondering how Basha managed to arrange such a huge amount in such a less time.

Shashi gets up, leaving his wife on floor and starts to argue with Basha.

"From where did you get this much money? Did you rob or something?" asked Shashi.

"No, my brother, I haven't robbed," replied Basha politely.

"Then how? Or did you get involved in some illegal activities?" asked Shashi in very condemning manner.

"It's a big story, please trust me, brother," said Basha passing his hand through his hair in a tense manner.

"Shashi, now is not the time to discuss how he got the money," said Parvathamma.

"You first pay the amount in the hospital. Brother, as of now, I can't explain how I got the amount," said Basha.

"First, I have to go to the police station and after returning, I will tell in detail," said Basha.

In a few seconds he departed from the hospital.

"He himself is having a huge credit on his auto rickshaw, so how did he get so much cash?" said one of the family members.

"Yes, that's true. How did he manage Rs. 10 lakhs?" murmured another family member.

"God only knows, we will come to know about this amount later, perhaps."

Basha departed from the hospital and headed to police station to handover the remaining money to the police. In the police station Basha confessed that he had used Rs. 10 lakhs of the total money for the hospital and that he was going to return the amount shortly.

Then S.I. Harish calls Rajath and narrates the whole story to him.

Rajath Kulkarni agreed that the kidnappers had divided the money into two bags. Rajath Kulkarni also came to know that Basha had used the money in the hospital. So Rajath, in light of Basha's good heart, donates another Rs. 2 lakhs to Basha and Rs. 2 lakhs for police welfare association and walks out with the remaining money.

The Story Ends

The story of the good-hearted Basha doesn't end here. This is only the beginning of a good ending. Shashi without knowledge had committed a mistake, but the repercussion of his action chased him and gave him the punishment. And he thinks that he hasn't done any mistake and blames it all on God. The truth is, it was the punishment for his mistake. And in another case, Basha has done good deed, which followed him and gave him and his family a fortune, making everyone happy, but everyone around him blames God for Basha's fortune. But the truth is that he was rewarded for his noble acts towards the nature and fellow beings. From this, I want to say that all good human beings reap good, and all bad human beings reap bad results. So do good activities and always think good and become good for yourself and to this world.

SPIRIT OF MOTHER EARTH

A long time ago, human beings believed that plants were non-living beings, but now man believes that plants are also living creatures in the same manner as most of the human beings. We humans think that trees do not have a soul, but the truth is that they do have a soul, very similar to that of human beings soul.

GOOD-HEARTED PEOPLE

The message that I want to give as an author, to the readers is very simple: Good things happens because of good actions, good thoughts, good gestures and good work. And bad things happen because of bad actions, irresponsibility, bad thoughts and carelessness. There is a saying - "A human being can choose anything in his life, but not his parents." It is up to God to choose the parents of a child. But this statement can be rewritten by human beings. Most of the human beings on this planet have the desire to be born as a billionaire's child or in royal families or in big political families. This desire can be fulfilled only through good actions. If any human being or living creature does good work, good actions and their work of responsibility which was assigned to them, then the human being or living creature have the option to choose the nature of their next birth. This option can be granted only by the spirit of "Mother Earth."

According to the good and bad actions (ancient astrology), Mother Earth allows us to choose our next birth. That doesn't mean doing good actions in one life and reincarnating in the next as a billionaire or in royal families or in big political families to enjoy a luxurious life. There comes more responsibilities with it. The "Spirits of Earth" promotes man for his good actions in one life to a billionaire in another, to take more responsibilities and do as many good deeds as possible. As the power of man increases, his responsibilities too increase proportionally. This is the way of nature.

So, I plead to the rich people, top politicians and literate people to do their work i.e., their responsibilities to the best of their capabilities or else we will have to face the consequences of not doing our responsibilities. Just by becoming rich or a top politician, doesn't mean you can enjoy life by exploiting your responsibilities. Instead, think that Mother Earth has just promoted you to the next level, to check on the performance of your work. If all of us fail in our responsibilities, then our Mother Earth will surely demote all of us.

There is some responsibility that Mother Earth has assigned to human beings, i.e., being the dominant species of this planet it is our duty to protect and conserve the plants, animals, water and natural resources of this planet. If we fail in our responsibilities, then we have to face the consequences such as epidemic diseases, incurable diseases, shortage of drinking water, rise in temperature, unnatural climate changes and natural calamities and ultimately the end of the humans and other species.

Mother Earth has helped us and this world evolve such that if a human being needs to survive on this planet, the condition is such that a certain group of animals, certain group of plants, certain percentage of atmospheric gases, layers, water must be there on this planet or else the living conditions of the human beings will be affected. Even if a single species of animal or plant gets extinct, then the consequences will be faced by human beings themselves.

Our Mother Earth is a very well-designed system in which every living organism and non-living organism is interconnected to each other, similar to the interconnectedness of a motorcycle, in which every small nut and bolt plays an important role in running the motorcycle. Without a bolt, the body of the motorcycle may collapse and the consequences have to be faced by the rider. Similarly, Mother Earth's system also needs well maintenance of its living and non-living organisms, or else we will have to face the consequences. Some of the consequences we are already facing; holes in ozone layer, melting of ice-caps and glaciers in Greenland and Antarctica, increase in the sea-level, increase in the temperature, rise in C02, decrease in drinking water, cancer and AIDS. Our Mother Earth's system is such that when there is a beginning for these diseases, there is also an end for the beginning. When there is a beginning for cancer and AIDS, then there is also a cure of these diseases. These diseases are the result of man's brutality against nature; otherwise these diseases would have been curable.

The medicine for many incurable diseases might have become extinct along with many extinct animals and plants. So, please play your part well in the responsibility assigned to us human begins i.e., to save, protect and conserve Mother Earth.

Everyone is this world, both theists and atheists want to see God. For the theist, seeing God is mainly to prove that God exists and make us believe in Him, to get rid of all the difficulties, and asking a boon to live in heaven. For atheists, seeing God is to prove and believe that God actually exists. Without seeing and experiencing, they don't believe in God. Before we proceed to see God, we must first know the qualities of God. Knowing the qualities of God, we will be able to see God and the Demon in our daily life.

QUALITIES OF GOD

1. God is the one who creates living and non-living organisms, to have a balanced life on this planet.
2. God is the one who protects living and non-living organisms to have a well-protected life on this planet.
3. God is the one who destroys the things which are against nature. Sometimes, even destruction is good for the beginning of a new life cycle.

4. God always does good things for good people and protects the good people. In Hinduism, natural resources like water, trees, animals rocks, space, earth and air etc., are also worshiped as gods. This is nothing but an attempt to conserve and protect natural resources, feed and protect the plants and animals. Hinduism is nothing but a science which explains the need for protection of natural resources, animals, plants and for the wellness of human beings. Anyone in this world who has qualities such as good character, good action, good manners, teaching good principles to the society, teaching the existence of truth, respecting the natural resources, animals, plants and fellow human beings and finally doing the work that is assigned to him, then that person may be considered as one among the gods. From this we can conclude that God exists in our actions. If it is a good action, then God can be seen, if it is a bad action then evil exists there. Finally, as an author, I wanted to say that the God and demons dwells in our hearts. It is up to us to unleash the God or demon through our actions. From this, I conclude that readers can see God in the mirror before going to bed.

Lord Ram, Lord Jesus, Lord Buddha, and Prophet Mohammed are worshiped as Gods in this world. Although these Gods were born as normal human beings, but they are worshiped as Gods because of their good actions, good character, teaching good principles to the society, teaching the principles of existence of truth. Even a normal human being will be worshiped, if they have the qualities of God.

Heaven and Hell

Every human being on this planet wants a place in heaven, but we human beings are not realizing that we already living in heaven. Till date, not a single human being has ever seen heaven, but many writers and holy books have described the nature of heaven. The same nature, plants, environment, climate and creatures are present on the earth, but we human beings are not realizing that and instead are converting and exploiting this heaven into hell. Everyone in the world wants to visit Dubai and Las Vegas once in their life time. These cities were once desert lands. These deserts were converted into heavenly cities by the citizens, politicians, and government authorities who did the work assigned to them. when a desert can be converted into such a beautiful city. Bangalore is already a heaven with the blessing of Mother Nature. It is our job to keep and maintain the city, thus making the city feel like heaven. There is yet time to save our city from getting polluted, so please do your duty efficiently.

GOD HAS CREATED A BEAUTIFUL HEAVEN, BUT WE HUMANS ARE CONVERTING THIS BEAUTIFUL HEAVEN INTO A HELL.

 # The ending credits

1. **Later one day, Narayan Mohan meets Basha, and takes him to meet Vijay, who has now become an owner of a mobile repair shop. Later, Vijay presents Basha with an advanced smart mobile set.**
2. **Knowing that there is a need for O -ve blood for Shiva, Karan Saxena donates his O -ve blood.**
3. **Karan Saxena and Pankaj become good friends.**
4. **Siddharth and Mukesh were imprisoned for five years.**
5. **Couple of months later, Kiran and Shwetha, and Praveen and Revathi, marry in a grand ceremony.**
6. **Shashi loses his job, because Praveen's company was somehow interconnected to Shashi's company.**
7. **Basha as usual rides his auto rickshaw with honesty, serving the people.**

8. **Few years later, Roopa Kulkarni wins the Miss World title. Later, she marries her longtime boyfriend Aditya Saxena (Academy award nominee).**
9. **Even after a 100 years, the tree which Basha saved, stands firm, providing shelter for humans, birds and animals.**